AF504518

Sailing the Golden Chersonese

Joyce Chng

QUEEN
of
SWORDS
PRESS

Contents

Sailing the Golden Chersonese

Joyce Chng

Acknowledgements

The book isn't possible without the help and support of friends and family in my life. Writing can be such a lonely path—support from loved ones is more invaluable than anything else. Thank you for gifting me the space and privilege to write, the time to dream, the voice to speak.

Many thanks to Catherine Lundoff, publisher of Queen of Swords Press, for giving this book a safe haven, a berth to call home.

Likewise, I see you, fellow travellers of the Golden Chersonese of our lives—may you find joy and wind in your sails, your Bintang Utara, as you sail the often-challenging seas. May your crew give you strength, surround you with kindness, and hold on to one another to ride out the waves.

May you also find safe ports and quiet seas.

Introduction

When I started writing *Saints and Bodhisattvas*, I didn't plan to turn it into a longer and more elaborate arc. I wanted to write something set in Southeast Asia. So, Kapitan Neo, Maria and Halim appeared in my mind, as well as the perahu *Sri Matahari*. A story of love, revenge and found family (of some sorts), and vows/choices.

The beginning of *Saints and Bodhisattvas* sounded like the introduction to a fable, a land of mystery and beauty. The name "Golden Chersonese" came from two sources: historical and a book written by Isabella L. Bird. The Malay Peninsula was indeed called the Golden Chersonese by Greek and Roman geographers. The name itself made it sound something out of a dream, a myth … while in reality, it exists. Furthermore, I thought about the influences that made the Chersonese into what it is. We have had migrations, colonizations, and the rise of empires. At the same time, there have been ongoing exchanges and cross-fertilizations of ideas, beliefs and faiths. The people of the Golden Chersonese adapted all these things and made them their own unique experiences. And by experiences, I mean they are lived-in and not stagnant. Southeast Asia is ever-changing even as I sit at my comfortable desktop.

I would say the Southeast Asia Neo and Maria are living in is a world of my re-visioning. Because it is, in a way, alternate history, I have taken the liberty of changing things. And I wanted to see a world that navigates its way via acts of empathy, kindness and compassion (I know, weird for a pirate tale). There is violence, but there is also the gentleness of love and healing, of tender embraces and love-making. There is mystical magic, but there is also the return to reality. Things are interwoven together, just as Southeast Asia sees its cultures often intertwined.

In this collection, the arc is complete. From *Saints and Bodhisattvas* to *Golden Beads and Eagle Wings*, we explore Neo and Maria's relationship as well as their place in the world, and how they confront the changes along the way.

I wrote with a Happy Ever After firmly in mind. At the time of writing this introduction, the world is burning. There is a lot of pain, distrust and anger. There is the feeling of despair and sheer helplessness. A HEA might not seem a lot—but it gives hope to people who do not feel that hope and the strength to persist.

So hold onto that hope, be that saint bodhisattva in someone's life. May your journey be lit with floating candles and nourishing broths.

Harimau mati meninggalkan belang, manusia mati meninggalkan nama.

(A tiger dies leaving behind its stripes, a person dies leaving his name.)

Andaman Sea
KAMPUCHEA
Gulf
of
Siam
SIAM
THAILAND
South China Sea
THE
GOLDEN
CHERSONESE
MALAY ARCHIPELAGO
Strait of Melaka
TEMASEK
ANDALUS
SUMATRA

Saints and Bodhisattvas

WHERE THE STRAITS INTERLACED each other with the confluences of currents and trade routes was the famed Golden Chersonese, a beacon of light, the center of all wealth and riches. Saints and bodhisattvas met there, allies in the inter-exchange of spirituality and learning. You would find your path there, they said. You would never hunger nor would you thirst. Bewitching creatures lurked in the Golden Chersonese, fantastic animals that populated your mind's bestiary. Birds of paradise with tails that flamed like the sun, dragons with large flickering tongues and poisonous saliva, and large cats that roared and founded a city. It lured many explorers, sailors of the sea and wind. It lured me.

I was born in the middle, a straddler between two worlds, one of the sea and one of solid land. The midwife laughed and said I was destined to ride the waves, breathing both ocean air and the sap of sea almond and angsana trees easily. Ibu was perturbed by the midwife's words, but she only held me, so she said, trying to protect me from the elements. I was in the middle, where the currents of life swirled like whirlpools forming at the wake of ships. At two, I was already swimming. At four, I stood at the prow of a skiff, the sea breeze on my face, the sea singing in my veins. At ten, I joined my father in his travels. I remembered soaring sunbaked stupas, the Sanskrit and Pali of saffron-robed monks, and the solemn tolling of gereja bells on Formosa's hill. I remembered the fragrance of spices and sandalwood wafting through the narrow sunbaked streets of Melaka, the cries of the vendors hawking their wares.

When I turned eighteen, I was given my own perahu. Rare for a girl, but I was never a girl, never a boy either. I wore a lacy kebaya at home, a simple chinon and baggy trousers at sea. My hair was bound tight. I swung on ropes, unencumbered by loose strands of hair. My right hand held a dao, a gift from a friend whom I saved. His ship burned, his cargo gone, but he lived. He was grateful to be alive. I was a saint for saving him.

I fought with his dao, now my dao. With it, I explored the Golden Chersonese.

Then, she came into my life like a bodhisattva.

MY MEN WERE LOUDLY discussing the merits of cooking while they repaired my ship. Away from home, they longed for their homes, so they distracted themselves with repair work. Sleek, sharp of prow, my ship cut through the sea like a kris. Yet it was not invincible against the forces of nature. Wood wore down easily, got chipped and sometimes dented. The underside of the ship had to be scraped thoroughly. Months at sea meant abundant growth of sea life. The sharp edges of the shells on the ship's sides hurt our exposed skin.

They joked about making seafood kari with the mussels as they removed them. On lean days we often picked them off the sides of the ship and ate them boiled in coconut water. I never liked them. I craved my mother's nasi ulam. I missed the cleansing taste of the finely-chopped herbs and the bitterness of the fried shallots. But to play along, I laughed with them, like the way my father had taught me. In their eyes, I was the towkay's son.

The last raid saw our rival, another band of lanun, trying to escape. In their panic, they rammed the prow of their perahu into the side of my ship. The sound of it made me sick to the stomach. It reminded me of breaking bones. We were lucky water hadn't seeped in. We limped into our port, our lives and cargo intact. I was livid. We would have to spend the whole month repairing the ship and miss a season of plying the sea before the torrential rains returned. I hated returning to port and having to wait the rains out. For the repairs, I traded in a new chest of precious Chinese silk in exchange for tools and timber. I had intended the chest to be sold to a buyer. It felt like a bad start to the season.

Around this time, the dry season was nearing its end, ready to go but unwilling to leave. The land was parched, the grass a brittle brown, and the wind hot against my cheeks. It blew in gusts, stirring up puffs of dust from the ground. A large desiccated spider tumbled across my sandaled feet. The withdrawing tide exposed the seabed rippling with life. Tiny fish darted in the pools of clear water. Crabs waved their pincer claws. I leaned back into the warm sand, my arm across my eyes, glad for some respite. I only wanted the repairs done as soon as possible. The heat lulled me into a light nap.

I heard someone walking towards me, footsteps crunching on the sand. I glimpsed beaded slippers with glittering beads of vivid red and green. Beaded slippers? I raised my face then to the glare of the afternoon sun. She stood before me, imperious, the sunlight outlining a slim figure clothed in a vivid sea-green kebaya and red sarong. Young nonyas were usually accompanied by a stern matronly chaperone when they left their house, if they ever left it at all. They led sheltered lives. What a rare occurrence indeed.

"You must be the captain of the *Sri Matahari*." The voice was young and confident, clear with precise pronunciation of the patois spoken in our parts of the Golden Chersonese. I got up quickly, dusting my chinon trousers as I surveyed the girl in front of me.

Her hair was a light brown. Under the sun, the strands shimmered gold. Her skin was the color of my own: the color of a Peranakan child— olive skin with subtle shades of perang. Her dark eyes were large and bright with a lively intelligence. Portuguese Kristang, then. There was a large population of them in this part of Melaka. They were mostly fishermen. The wealthier ones ran shipping consortiums.

"I am," I said briskly.

"I have a request . . . a job for you," the young woman continued without any introduction. "I will pay you."

I smiled wryly. "I won't agree to any request without knowing the name of my potential hirer."

Her full lips twitched. She must have pouted a lot as a child. She schooled her irritation with a smile too. "I am Maria."

"What can I do for you, Maria?" I stifled my own chuckle. She must have thought I was a man.

She leaned forward suddenly, her manner at once shy and conspiring. Something flashed bright at her neck. A silver necklace. "I want you to kill a man."

"Kill a man?"

I raised an eyebrow. I had encountered such requests before and twice I refused them very politely. I wasn't an assassin.

"Captain Neo," Maria said severely.

"So you do know my name. Back to my question: Kill a man?"

"Not so loud!" the young woman snorted. My first mate, Halim, looked up sharply. He was always alert and quick to respond. That was why he was my father's first mate and now mine. Only he knew who I actually was.

"I am not a killer." I shook my head.

"You are lanun. Lanun kill people," Maria pushed on. I frowned. I was beginning to dislike her attitude. I wanted her to go away. "You are not averse to killing."

"You must have mistaken me for something I am not. I am just a simple trader," I said very mildly. My men knew that particular tone very well. Suddenly, all repair work stopped and the men stood up, very slowly, with hands on their parangs and kris knives, glaring darkly at her. "You have such a low opinion of us. We are not the ruffians you think we are."

"Ai meu Deus!" Maria said angrily. She had noticed their reaction. She was no fool.

"I know that expression, senhora. You don't have to swear."

"I would like you to hunt down the man who killed my father," Maria whispered, her voice harsh, almost guttural. Her eyes were wet with unshed tears and she clearly hated showing that weakness in front of me and my men. "I know who and what you really are. *Please help me.*"

Her voice tugged at something in me. Loss. Pain. Despair. I thought of my father, already several years dead. He died when I was twenty, a victim of the prolonged coughing sickness.

"*Please.* Que os santos te abençoem."

May the saints bless you. I knew the phrase. All the captains who plied the Golden Chersonese learned the two or three languages spoken at the major and minor ports, besides the "port tongue" which was a mixture of all the languages together. I glanced at the silver necklace on her neck. It was a small crucifix. Serani. Most of the Portuguese Kristang were called Serani by the rest.

Against my better judgment, I nodded.

HER FULL NAME WAS Maria Fernandes.

Once she was perceived as nonthreatening, my men went back to repairing the ship, their voices loud enough to be heard from the deck where I invited Maria for freshly brewed Ceylon tea. I did so because it was the right way to show hospitality to guests, and because this was the way my father had taught me. It was also a good way to gauge my guest face-to-face, over tea and preserved sweetmeats from my own personal store.

Maria took off her slippers to walk up the wooden plank, even mincing daintily across without losing her balance. She politely declined my helping hand to step into the ship. Her sarong restricted her movements, yet she moved quickly and with grace. Soon, she sat, legs tucked under her, while I poured the tea into delicate porcelain cups. They were the craze at the moment, all the way from China. She nibbled on the sweetmeats, complimenting the taste of the sugared dry hawthorn. I sipped my tea, wondering who she really was, where her family lived.

"I am an orphan," she said without being prompted. "If you are curious as I think you are. I was adopted by a Peranakan family . . . but I left on amiable terms. This kebaya and sarong . . . they belong to a friend who took me in." She lapsed into silence, staring into the sea. Heat shimmered over the horizon. The sky was a clear blue.

"Ah, I see," I said. "How will you pay me? This is a business transaction."

She looked up, her eyes wide, her nostrils flaring. I realized she was afraid. "I will . . . pay you once the deed is done. In the meantime, please grant me permission to work onboard your ship."

"This is still very vague, Maria. I can't work on the basis of empty terms. My men need payment. Let me remind you that we are all rough people." I shook my head. "We are all used to rough and hard work."

Maria stared hard at me. "I have heard rumors about you, that you are actually a woman in disguise. I can work just as hard as a man."

"What if I am?" I challenged back, suddenly

angry at the intrusion of my privacy. Rumors were often spread by jealous gossip and idle chatter. "Can you handle a weapon? Will you faint at the sight of blood?"

"No!" Her shout startled me with its sheer vehemence. "I am not some fragile flower! If it's handling weapons you want, I can do it. Teach me!" She spat the words out as if they bothered her.

"Well, then," I said finally. "My ship's still being repaired. We can't leave immediately."

"I can wait," Maria pouted. "Even if it means a month."

Halim chose this time to pop up, peering straight into the ship at us. He was a wiry man, built for the sea. Age had grizzled his temples, but his eyes were still sharp, his tongue even sharper. I saw him as a father of sorts, a replacement for my own. He wore his customary dark sarong and left his torso bare. His family kris hung by his side. "Adakah semua dalam keadaan yang baik?" he asked, glancing at Maria sternly. Maria glared back, unafraid.

"We are well," I smiled, waving him away. "Don't worry."

My first mate nodded curtly and ducked back out into the afternoon sun, shouting orders to the crew to stop lazing round. Maria left her tea untouched. "I have no family left," she said.

"We will talk more tomorrow," I said, suddenly

tired. Maria's presence had stirred emotions I'd thought were gone. I missed my own family.

I WOKE UP FROM a dream where my mother was making sambal with the batugiling. Her strong hands rolled the stone cylindrical pestle across the large mortar board. I could hear the stone grinding against the chili and herbs. Somewhere, someone was singing. The smell of the chopped galangal and chili being mixed intoxicated me. My heart ached with longing. I opened my mouth to say something to my ibu . . . only to peer up, sore and ill-rested, at the ceiling of my cabin.

I found Maria waiting for me at the bottom of the ship, on the shore next to the vessel. It was barely morning yet. The tide had rolled in and the hint of rain was in the air. The men slept in, wrapped in their sarongs. Only Halim seemed awake. He was idly fishing, but I knew he was also alert and listening for any sign of trouble.

She had not slept. She was still wearing her kebaya and was wrapped in a tattered shawl. I glanced down at her feet. Bare. The beaded slippers were gone.

"Are you comfortable?" I asked. Maria smiled wanly at me. "We walk barefoot on the ship. Are you sure you don't need protection for your feet?" My own were callused from years onboard ships.

She only nodded. The sky was beginning to lighten. A sliver of golden orange peered over the east. Was Maria the kind to bolt? Time to seal the agreement. I spat into my right hand and extended it to Maria. Without hesitation, she spat into her right palm and then pressed it against mine. She didn't even flinch.

"Your life is now mine and my life is now yours," I intoned the formal phrase used amongst people of our particular trade. "You share your food with us and we share our food with you. We eat the same food. We breathe the same air. The sea protects you and me."

"Amém," Maria said, crossing herself. My lips quirked. I decided I was going to like her.

"Let's break fast." I walked towards Halim, who had started a fire to grill the ikan kuning he'd caught. "And let us get you something to wear. That finery has to go."

"Please let me keep the kebaya." Maria hurried to join me. "I want to remember something from my former life."

"Of course," I answered coolly. The cooking fish smelled delicious.

WE FOUND HEADGEAR, A plain grey chinon and dark green trousers for Maria. The headgear came from Halim's own pile of clothing, the chinon and trousers from my chest since we shared a similar body type. Divested of her kebaya and sarong, Maria looked like a boy in her new clothes, her hair tied up into a tight bun and hidden under the headgear. She wore no weapon yet. Her necklace still hung on her neck.

She ate with what seemed like a healthy appetite, picking the flesh off the fish bone with her fingers and chewing the whole fish head before chasing it down with more Ceylon tea.

"The ship's not ready yet," Halim reported. "We need one day more."

"Our men are hardworking," I said. My first mate grinned, a flash of white teeth.

"They are motivated by the sea," he said, before leaning closer, darting a quick look at Maria, who was still ignored by the rest of the men who swarmed over the ship. "You trust *her?*"

"Hers is a blood feud. She seeks revenge."

"Keep an eye on her, Kapitan. I would rather have her off the ship."

"She has no family."

Halim snorted. "That's the reason given by half of our men. And . . . she's . . . you know . . . a woman . . ." He let the sentence trail into silence.

"You said that about me a long time ago."

"You are our towkay's child."

"Son. Our towkay's *son.*"

Halim's face reddened. "Kapitan, you proved yourself on the sea. Her? I am not sure, though I have heard that there are women on the other ships too, just as fierce and bloodthirsty as men."

"Let her go clean the ship's deck first," I said

finally, wrapping my headgear around my head. "That's her first test."

By midday, Maria hung around like a bedraggled ghost. The ship floor was scrubbed but she was thorough.

"Not bad," Halim said, sounding unconvinced.

"Let her mend the sails," I said.

By evening, she sat, looking pale. The sails were mended, the tears neatly sewn. She managed to get the tools from the men, who treated her as some sort of novelty. Halim made seafood kari, the spices courtesy from our own supplies, the fish and shrimp netted from the day's catch. Maria received her coconut husk-bowl of kari and retreated to the prow of the ship, where she ate alone.

"Now let us see if she decides to stay," I nibbled at my own food.

I WAS WOKEN UP by the sound of splashing water and the smell of cooking fire. I peered out from my cabin. Maria was boiling water in the tin kettle. Fish was already cooking on wooden skewers she picked from the fallen twigs beneath the portia trees. She had caught enough for all of us.

I smiled.

SRI MATAHARI CUT THROUGH the water, as if relieved to be released from confinement. Her sails caught the wind full. I heard them humming their familiar song. Around me, the men went about their usual duties, checking the ropes, the hooks, and sharpening their weapons. Halim stood at the lookout, his eyes watching everything. Our pilot, Abdullah, steered the rudder. He had an intuitive touch when it came to guiding the ship.

"Maria!" I barked.

She ran up quickly. Her eyes sparkled. I could feel her excitement. So far she had shown no sea-sickness. She didn't seem to mind the sea. Perhaps, somewhere in her blood, there was seawater.

"Where does the murderer of your father live?" I asked.

"Temasek," she replied quickly, her voice cold. "He lives on Temasek."

WHILE SRI MATAHARI SAILED, I taught Maria basic weapon drills. I couldn't possibly teach her all the things I knew. Instead, I chose one weapon and stuck to it. Maria handled the dagger easily. Block, attack, strike. Block, attack, strike. I knew the men watched the practice from the corner of their eyes, still painfully polite and reluctant to engage her with their activities.

"You need to be more aggressive," I pushed her. "Attack me. The people you meet later will not be nice nor will they be gentle."

Maria gritted her teeth. She had stopped pouting. In fact, I had not seen her pout since she came aboard. She came at me, her guard open. I stepped aside and twisted her arm. She struggled.

"Again," I said. I released her. She didn't rub her arm. Instead, she inhaled deeply, closing her eyes, before opening them again. She rushed, I evaded, only to have her sidestep me. Her foot caught me off-balance. I tripped and stumbled. The men chuckled.

She reached down to help me up. Her grip was strong. I got to my feet. I could smell Maria. She smelled of spices and sweat. Her hair oil was not unpleasant, her body soft and warm. I felt my body respond, a flush of moist heat between my legs. The response surprised me. I had never felt like this before.

Before I could speak, she had placed her dagger onto my bare neck. I felt the cold edge press gently against the skin. "Surprise," she whispered in my ear. "You have thick soles. I think you need shoes." She smirked.

"Beginner's luck." I pulled away, scowling at her. "Well done and thank you, no, I don't."

HALIM SIGHTED THE SHIP from a distance.

We were nearing Temasek, having navigated the complex network of small islands and sandy shoals surrounding the island. Maria had spent the week on the ship learning how to steer the rudder, wrestle and hone her fighting skills, and scrub the deck with coconut-husk bristles. The week had passed uneventfully. The season had only begun. Most ships would only emerge from their hideouts and ports once the merchant ships arrived. The ones plying the straits now were either fishermen or. . . people like us.

I had grown used to watching Maria prepare hot water and food every morning. I grappled with the surge of emotions and physical sensations whenever I saw her. I dreaded and craved standing next to her. She was the saint I couldn't bear to touch, a bodhisattva so holy I felt guilty for even walking close to her. An exquisite and rare beautiful bird-of-paradise. Yet, she saw me as her captain and the person whom she had hired to kill her father's murderer. The voice of reason in me warned me to stay far away from her and maintain an air of business. I had never had a woman onboard my ship. Halim was right. It stirred up *things* in me. I had sworn to be alone. People would never understand who and what I was.

Her presence was trouble.

The men were not immune either. One by one, they started to drift close to her, so that they could catch a glimpse of her before scuttling away with their dignity intact. A couple of them tried to share food with her. When she washed herself with the clean water we stored in barrels, everyone pretended not to see. We draped a sheet across her part of the ship to cordon off the area. Yet she didn't seem interested in any of the men. She treated them like older brothers. Strange and distant older brothers.

Kill the murderer, get my payment, and we would be rid of her. These thoughts filled my head.

Where would she go once the deed was done?

"Perahu!" Halim shouted.

It slid in confidently, like a hunting shark lured by blood and the prospect of a meal. The perahu was of the same make as *Sri Matahari*. Its sails were angled sharply. The captain was banking on speed. There were lanun who prided themselves on their attack skills. Many were hit-and-run experts: attack their opponent or merchant, take what they needed, kill everyone aboard. I had seen ships adrift at sea, the crew dead and the cargo stolen. Most of the time, we just sailed past and offered a prayer.

What else could we do?

There were ten figures standing at the side of the ship, their weapons drawn. They were ready to board. Their pilot was steering the perahu so that it was heading at us directly. They were ready to board and kill. Abdullah yanked at the rudder and *Sri Matahari* moved, pulling away. It was our own tactic, to draw the enemy into a circling dance. "Let them give chase," I said, my heart pounding. I relished the taste of the hunt. My blood was singing in my veins. Beside me, Maria swallowed convulsively. Her eyes widened.

The lanun drew close, enough to see their

features. Their faces showed a range of colors: perang and putih. There were three Dutch men among them. Some of the Dutch decided to stay after incursions into the area. Most had moved to Batavia, where I heard they wreaked havoc and were terrible masters. They had fought with the Portuguese for territory: local rulers used them as pawns in their own bid to power. These Dutch men looked battle-hardened, their skin thick and leathery, their eyes fierce. They wore the same clothing with the rest. They had thrown in their lot with these lanun.

"Short sabers," Halim muttered darkly. "Probably stolen." He hated the Dutch.

Maria gripped her dagger with a wild look on her face. She seemed to have seen something . . . someone on the ship.

"What's wrong, Maria?" I said.

"It's *him*. I recognize him. He's there on the ship!" Her voice trembled, halfway between fear and exhilaration.

"Who's he?" I growled.

"My father's killer. One of the white men! There, look, he's wearing headgear!"

I saw him. He was a middle-aged man with white hair and a grizzled face. Tall and lanky, he leaned heavily to his left. Old injury?

"They fought over something a long time ago. They were . . . friends. He killed Papa. He killed him and Mama pined to her death. I saw her die.

I was only ten. *Ten.* I want to kill him for what he did to Papa and Mama. He destroyed my family!" Maria's voice was soft; her knuckles were white, her breathing shallow. Her eyes, though, blazed with hatred.

"Are you sure?" Halim snapped.

"Yes!" she shivered. Now she sounded flint-hard. "Yes!"

"You ready?" I asked her. "Are you sure?" I repeated Halim's question.

"Yes, I am."

"Abdullah, we are going in," I shouted.

Abdullah needed no further instruction. *Sri Matahari* began her attack run.

"Today you get to kill him and avenge them," I said.

WE DREW CLOSE ENOUGH to board. The lanun yelled curses at us. My men hurled the boarding hooks.

With a laugh, I leaped across, my dao aimed at the captain of the ship.

He was an old man, even older than Halim, but he fought harder than a cornered harimau. Still, I managed to subdue him, kicking him hard in the ribs. He fell hard backwards, his head hitting the boards. Dark blood seeped beneath the head. His men roared, having witnessed the death of their captain. They were going to fight even more viciously now.

In the tumult of combat, I didn't see Maria. Everybody was busy killing or not getting themselves killed.

The chaos parted to reveal Maria confronting the Dutchman who killed her father. Her eyes screamed death. She yelled a stream of Portuguese words so obscure I didn't understand most of them. Only "death" and "go to hell" made sense.

The man seemed to freeze, as if he recognized her, before he launched into a series of slashing cuts to drive her off. He wanted to kill her.

Maria ducked, dodging the saber. The silver necklace swung, catching the light of the sun. Then my line of vision was hindered by a tumbling mess of wrestling men. When they rolled away, I looked desperately for Maria. What I saw sent shocks up my back.

They were both on the deck and the Dutchman had her pinned to the floor, his saber tip pointed towards her throat. She was resisting him as fiercely and strongly as she could, spitting into his face. He swore and cursed at her. Suddenly, he grunted and his entire body stiffened. Maria had somehow managed to shove her dagger deep in his chest.

"Go to hell," I heard her say in Portuguese. The man didn't respond. He was already dead. She looked disgusted as she pushed the corpse off her body and pulled the dagger out of its chest. There was a deep hole, welling quickly with thick red heart's blood.

By this time, the battle was done. The remaining crew members begged for mercy, only to have Halim slit their throats with his kris. The rest of my men went about the dead bodies, making sure the crew remained dead. The ship was carrying stolen cargo: three boles of expensive Chinese silk and two large cedar-wood chests. Upon opening the chests, we found eighty gold and silver ingots in each. They must have recently attacked a merchant ship to have such riches. We were in luck. I thanked all the deities, even the saints and bodhisattvas. I was already planning to give some of the gold to ibu on my next visit to my family home.

Dagger in hand, Maria stood in the sea of corpses, staring numbly at the dead men, including the body of her father's killer.

"It's done," she said in a soft voice. "Rest in peace, Papa and Mama."

She didn't cry. After wiping her dagger clean of blood, she helped the men carry the cargo across the plank, back to our ship.

We left the perahu adrift, the fate of every lanun who died at sea. *Sri Matahari* sailed away, richer and heavier.

"I am voiding our agreement," I told Maria when the ship found shelter at a quiet mangrove swamp. Halim was wading in the soft mud, ready to hunt for the large meaty crabs. We would celebrate later with a meal of boiled mud crab.

"Why? I promised to pay you," Maria sputtered. She seemed to have weathered her first kill well.

"We have two chests of ingots. I am going to give you eight of the gold ones. I hope you can start a new life with them."

"Eight gold ones." Maria let her words trail off.

"We will drop you back in port tomorrow," I said. "Go back to your friend. Pay her one gold ingot as compensation."

"No, I want to stay," Maria said firmly. "I want to stay on the ship. With you."

"I am not your protector."

"You are not," Maria said. "But we swore an oath, remember? *Your life is now mine and my life is now yours.*"

"Ah."

"I want to uphold our oath," she said, watching Halim catch his first mud crab. He was chuckling away like a little boy with his first catch, his face and legs smeared with mud. The men laughed too. It had been a bountiful day.

"I want to travel the Golden Chersonese with the ship . . . with you," she continued, her gaze returning to rest on me. She was very close now. I could smell her. She'd washed herself thoroughly with our water after the encounter with the lanun. She bore the fragrance of sea salt. Her dagger rested tucked in her belt. "I want to know you better," she said shyly.

My heart rose at those words. I tried to maintain a stern demeanor. "You might get more than what you bargained for."

"The Peranakan matriarch bitch made me do all the menial chores," Maria snorted. "I can cook. I can sweep the deck. I can sew. I can endure *anything*."

"Anything? Including me? I can be rather unbearable, just ask Halim," I replied. "Are you sure?"

"You are interesting, Captain Neo," Maria giggled. "I can endure you."

"I am only *interesting?*" My heart did a small leap: she could endure me.

Maria laughed her first real laugh. Such a wonderful sound. The men glanced quickly at her, startled by her sudden gaiety.

"Of course." Her eyes sparkled merrily. "That is why I want to know you better." Her hand brushed mine, such a feathery and yet still-startling touch. I jumped, but my hand touched her back.

"Indeed," I said. "Indeed."

So, YOU CAME INTO my life like a bodhisattva. We sailed the Golden Chersonese together, you and me, straddlers between the worlds. With two of the gold ingots, I bought you a pair of new boots, no more beaded slippers, but in the latest fashions outside the Golden Chersonese. They were apparently the rage in the courts of the kings and queens. They were made of the finest leather, with the tracery of yellow flower embroidery curling along the edges and the softest of velvet lining their insides. You laughed and said you could run faster with bare feet. "Don't be silly," you said as the sun rose above us in reds and oranges.

I laughed back. You kept the shoes in your private wooden box with the kebaya and sarong. You still wore your silver necklace.

And all was right in the world again.

Silks and Celadon

Sri Matahari flew above the waves, her sharp bow cutting through the waters like a silver blade. The sea breeze bore the hint of salt and painted our skin with moisture. Her flight was joined by the flitting shapes of flying fish leaping out of the water.

We were fresh from a raid, the perahu's hold filled with chests and boxes of treasures and precious goods. My blood was still up, hot and coursing through my veins. I stood beside Abdullah, my helmsman, my face towards the setting sun now a ball of deep yellow sinking into the western horizon. It was a good raid, a good hunt—the men needed the boost to their morale. Their cheers lifted my spirits too.

The pickings had been lean, of late, as the western powers had strengthened their patrols, threatening the livelihoods of lanun and boatsmen in the Golden Chersonese. Too many of their laden galleons were raided and they felt the pinch in their pockets. Their merchants, proud and arrogant, clamored for protection. These patrols had guns and cannons. Our smaller perahus were defenseless against such weaponry.

Still, the chests in *Sri Matahari's* hold were a reassurance that lanun could still hunt on the seas. The sea was still ours. The silk fabrics promised riches.

I glanced over to check on Maria, who smiled back brightly, her face like the sun coming back after rain. Dressed like one of us, she looked like a slim boy. She was cleaning her dagger with a strip of cloth.

She had taken well to the life of a lanun and life at sea. Halim had grudgingly accepted the fact she was a faster runner than he was. They often cooked the meals for the men, Halim being a master at foraging while Maria learned by watching him. She had picked up the ways to identify edible fish, plants and roots. Her first success was the netting of the big mud crabs that often made mangrove banks their home. In turn, she became an expert on how to clean and cook the crabs.

"Have you eaten flying fish?" Halim asked Maria once.

"No?" Maria's eyes were wide. In some ways still, she was extremely sheltered.

"They are good grilled over fire," Halim said, his eyes twinkling. "We catch them like insects . . .

with nets . . . Their eggs are delicious too, if you ferment them in salt and vinegar long enough."

I chuckled when I saw Maria's look of surprise. It was close to the evening meal and we were growing hungry.

Abdullah found a secluded cove through an inlet. The men leaped off the perahu, securing the ship, and prepared for the night, lighting a small fire. Halim brought out the silver pots to make a soup with anything he could find.

I allowed the men some arak. They earned it. As the orange-pink skies darkened and the stars began to emerge, someone took out a mouth harp and began playing a tune. The cove was silent; we were far from villages and cities. There were the sound of waves and the sigh of the sea breeze. The tune filled the air with a sense of longing.

I OPENED THE CHESTS and boxes. I knew two contained the silk fabrics. The boxes held celadon vases, made by masters. Their color was sublime—the layers of deep ocean or the greenest green of the lalang grass. They would still fetch a hefty sum in the markets. My spirits soared. We could eat (well) for a while.

"Hey." Maria quietly slid into the hold. The rest of the men were asleep, with Abdullah and Halim on watch. They were smoking cheroots and talking softly about home.

I allowed Maria to snuggle against me as I

closed the chests. Her warmth was delicious; I savored her scents of coconut oil and jasmine. I gave her a vial of special perfume, that of jasmine oil, a few moons ago. She cherished the vial and used it sparingly. Just a dab behind the ears and on the neck. Enough to drive me to distraction and arousal.

"We can finally eat," I said. "Silks and celadon."

"Nonsense, we can always eat." Maria gestured playfully at the water. "We can fish. I can find edible leaves and seaweed."

I laughed aloud. Halim flung a quick glance at us, before looking away. I swore he had a smile on his lips.

"We can use some of the currency now, and buy you treats. And *Sri Matahari* needs repairs. Riau Islands have some of the best shipwrights." I pushed the boxes and chests to one side. The hold was a cramped space, but it served as our sleeping "room." I laid out the mats and batik cloth used as our blankets. With one single candle providing golden light and cloth serving as a screen, it was our private space. We curled up against each other, Maria stroking my chest as we slowly fell asleep to the sound of the sea.

AFTER A MORNING MEAL of hot white rice (Halim kept a small tin of rice grains) and leftover soup, we readied the perahu for another day at sea. Halim harvested young coconuts to be kept onboard the ship. Their water was cool and refreshing, while the meat was crisp and sweet. Sailing was thirsty work.

At last, the men pushed *Sri Matahari* off into the water. No longer clumsy on dry land, *Sri Matahari* moved as if she had wings. Her sails billowed with the strong sea wind. In the past, *Sri Matahari's* smaller kin raced each other with colorful sails. They were so unlike the large galleons that seemed to wallow in the water. I looked forward to another successful hunt.

The sea seemed unusually quiet.

There should be lanun and honest fishermen out by now. Yet I saw none, save for one or two smaller perahus that sped away the moment they saw *Sri Matahari*.

"They look like fish afraid of a shark," Halim commented pointedly. "Something is amiss, Kapitan. I do not like it."

I had been kapitan long enough to feel the peculiar twinge in my gut. Halim was right: something did not feel right.

"Ship!" the lookout yelled.

It emerged from the heat shimmer like one of the ghost ships I had heard so much about. *Ghost ships*. Ships that sailed without a crew. I shivered, even with the sun on my skin. I stared harder. I recognized the shape and make of the ship.

A galleon!

"Ready your weapons," I yelled.

IT WAS NOT A ghost ship. It had a crew, a brave captain and his first mate. Their accents gave them away: a crew of English and Dutch men. Maria was no doubt disturbed. A Dutchman killed her father. The same cold anger gripped her as she went about stabbing her dagger into the necks of the sailors. Halim and I had taught her well.

We took their cargo and left the ship adrift. It was surprising they were travelling without an escort. Halim looked at me knowingly. Perhaps some merchants felt brave enough not to travel with escorts and only armed themselves to the teeth. We took their weapons too; their rapiers and sabers too would fetch a sum in the black markets.

They were carrying three boxes of opium, two boxes of Madeira wine, and three chests of brocade. Expensive goods indeed, especially the opium, which was a narcotic used by men and women. My skin crawled. I did not like substances like these. The men and women grew tied to the opium, unable to liberate themselves from such cruel oppression. They grew sick of the body and the mind.

"The dark substance," Halim noted grimly. "They are plying in such trade."

"Earns them currency," I said. "They also have lanun amongst their midst." I had heard enough: pirate, buccaneer and, most recently, privateer. They hunted on behalf of their respective governments.

The politics of the western powers were as complicated as a spider's web.

"We can dump them elsewhere," Halim groused.

"And have someone else find it and have it then sold? The cycle continues." I shook my head. "Somewhere someone grows the plant that gives this dark substance. Somewhere someone is caught in that same cycle."

"You sound like some arhat." Halim grinned. "Some holy man who lives close to the temples."

"I am not," I said. "You decide where the boxes should go."

In the end, Halim had the boxes sunk to the bottom of the sea. It had been a rule of this perahu to have no opium onboard. The men were all aware of this rule. Instead, now we consoled ourselves with the wine and the brocade. The shimmering fabric was destined to be made into some finery for a highborn lady. Maria had brocade boots, a gift from me. I had a vision of Maria in brocade. What a fine figure she would make.

Barefoot, Maria walked up to me. "It was still a good raid," she said.

I nodded. I was not able to shake the feeling of disquiet. It had hung around like a feral dog hungry for scraps.

We docked at one of the closest islands. Currency was exchanged, goods were sold. We were thriving. I soon ignored the dark feeling. I was looking forward to paying the men, Halim, ship repairs and buying Maria some gifts. A lanun could dream big sometimes.

THE ISLAND'S ONLY VILLAGE—A cluster of wooden houses built on mussel-encrusted stilts—had a small market where merchants who had anchored at the bay met to sell their goods. Some of the merchants were also lanun I was friends with. They spoke about the increased patrols and how they had barely managed to escape from the cannons. The ships were faster than the galleons they were protecting. The shipwrights called them frigates. They all shared the same warning and foreboding: *be careful of these frigates.*

With the warning in mind, we set off once more. *Sri Matahari* had some silks, brocade and celadon left. We sold off the Madeira to a Melakan trader who doubled as a lanun in his spare time. He knew some clients who would appreciate such wines.

The warning was sobering and the feeling of disquiet returned. I busied myself with the maps, while Maria taught some of the men a dance. She was supposed to practice with her dagger. The men laughed. To her, they were like older (and distant) brothers. The men kept their distance. They knew she was the kapitan's—out of their league and totally hands off.

I tried to distract myself by checking the maps.

We were sailing close to the Riau Islands, close to Temasek. More ships plied there, given the fact that Temasek served as a major port, next to Melaka.

More patrols.

We would assume the identity of a small-time merchant or trader, changing the color of our sails to that of a merchant's. Time to keep our heads down. Assume innocence.

It was near high noon, when the sun shone directly above our heads and when the heat was so unbearable, the frigate appeared.

"Kapitan!" the lookout shouted.

The frigate bore down on us without mercy. It moved with terrifying speed, its sails catching the wind. It was indeed faster than the rotund galleons. Faster, lighter . . . and armed to the teeth. It bore no distinguishing flag, which was a worrying sign by itself.

"Pretend we are merchants on the way to Temasek," I said. In a way, it was true: we could find refuge at Temasek.

We waved the sails, signaling that we were just traders. The frigate did not seem to care.

Something whizzed overhead, barely missing the mast. It hit the water like an explosion. I soon learned how to hate the sound: a cannonball flying in the air.

"They are firing at us," Halim said, holding his kris, ready to fight. "They know who we are."

"Turn around," I spat. "We run."

Sri Matahari spun, Abdullah steering both wheel and rudder. The sail caught the wind, and *Sri Matahari* flew forward, seemingly to relish the sheer power of freedom. The hunt was on.

The hunter was now the hunted.

THE FRIGATE PURSUED US relentlessly. It had become a cat-and-mouse game or a sea-eagle-and-fish dance. When I was a child, my father brought me to the big marketplace in Java where everything was sold. There were indigenous tribesmen who had tamed and trained lang siput, the blue-grey sea-eagles, to hunt. The birds with hooked beaks perched on their tattooed bare arms, their sharp talons covered in wooden tubes. The tubes were from porous cork-like tree bark. The birds' keen eyes missed nothing and remained unwavering as their handlers cooed at them with affection. It was a mark of adulthood to be able to train an eaglet.

I felt as if *Sri Matahari* was under such scrutiny now. The frigate had eagle eyes. We were its prey. As soon as we slipped away, we found ourselves back as a hunted animal. I was beginning to think that the captain of the frigate might have a vendetta against me. It was that feeling of disquiet, the dark current I was used to. Danger, danger, danger. Was the captain some buccaneer or a privateer, sent by some shadowy power to hunt me down? I had made enough enemies.

It seemed to know how to navigate through

the many inlets and islands of the Riau Islands. I wanted to hide. I had some locations I had used when I hid from bigger lanun and the larger merchant ships. Would the frigate's captain know that too? I glanced at Halim, and then to Maria who nodded solemnly. Her courage gave me the strength to continue.

When the afternoon sky edged toward dusk, *Sri Matahari* found herself surrounded by small islands. I recognized them. One or two had villages on them and sheltered lanun. I glanced around. We had lost the frigate.

We slipped through the darkness, into an inlet overgrown with mangroves and nipah palms. I had hoped the thorns of the nipah palms and the intricate exposed roots of the mangroves would act as a natural defensive barrier. Not all the foreign captains had local knowledge of the islands.

In darkness, we hid, daring not to light candles in case we were spotted by some sharp-eyed sailor. In darkness, we chewed on young coconut meat and drank the clear sweet juice. Halim handed out dried salted fish. Normally eaten with hot white rice, it soon became our dinner. I chewed on the fish; it was still extremely salty and I winced a little, wishing for something bland to balance the taste in my mouth. Maria did not complain. She had grown used to the life of a lanun. She held my hand gently, a kind and loving presence.

We all huddled onboard the perahu

that night. She rocked gently with the waves. Somewhere in the distance, we could hear the azan—call to prayer—thin and reedy. Somewhere life carried on as usual.

And we knew somewhere the frigate was still searching for us.

ONE OF THE MEN went climbing through the roots and spiky palm trunks at first light to scout. He came back, panting, with bad news: "The ship is there, Kapitan. Like a hunting shark."

I cursed aloud. The frigate had us blocked. Who was the captain working for? Why this single-minded focus?

Why us?

It was due to the astuteness of Abdullah who managed to navigate through the small river leading to the sea that we managed to sail away. The feeling of freedom filled my being. The men cheered loudly. We kept to the islets, hugging the mangrove shores. I felt like prey trying to hide from the harimau. The beast was lurking close by; I could feel the frigate's presence like a looming shadow. It hunted us, surely, just as we were determined to evade its closing claws.

We crept into Selat Tebrau and lowered our sail. The Orang Laut welcomed us and gave us shelter. Honest boat folk, the Orang Laut lived their lives in and on the sea. They were also fearsome raiders, their expertise sought by many lanun. Their knowledge of the sea made them extremely valuable to the many kingdoms in the Golden Chersonese.

We were also close to Temasek, though proximity to the island did not give me reassurance. The frigate was still out there. We were still being pursued.

"You are hunted," the headman was blunt. He was an older man, the same age as Halim, perhaps even older. He was an acquaintance, an ally I had found many years ago. Father was his old friend. I called him Pakcik or Uncle.

"Yes, a frigate hunts us," I said. "A foreign ship without identifying flags."

"Patrol ships," Pakcik said, rubbing his chin. He then lit a cheroot. "The orang asing want their trade routes protected for their own purposes." Orang asing. Foreigners.

"So they do."

"Portuguese, English and Dutch." Pakcik blew smoke rings into the air. "They come in waves. I fear they take over the lands and seas in time."

I was chilled to the bone by this statement. I controlled the inevitable shudder. I must not show weakness!

"Some of our own," Pakcik handed me a cheroot which I accepted respectfully, "some of our own now work for them. They say they value our expertise. What expertise? This is our place, our sea. We know the sea as we know our own bodies. They only want to use us for their own gain."

"Could it be possible that one works for the frigate's master?" I lit the cheroot and sucked on it, exhaling thoughtfully. The cheroot had a musky, woody taste to it. I had tried not to get too used to cheroots. They had the same effect as opium.

"Surely when I can count the boats and fish before me," Pakcik said. The sampans and smaller perahus bobbed before us. The strait was calm, the water a serene light green, almost transparent. I could see small silver fish darting about in the sea grass. Needlefish wove in and out of the grass. There was almost a lesson there, the fish and sea grass. Pakcik often spoke in riddles and allusions to the sea. That was what Father sounded like. Metaphors, analogies, examples.

Pakcik's wife cooked us a simple meal of ground fresh red chili, grilled ikan kuning and hot white rice. Makcik made sure we all ate and with generous portions of rice. Pakcik gave the men tobacco and papers so that they could make their own smokes. I knew that the tobacco came from his private stash. The smokes were a mark of his hospitality. In turn, I also received the tobacco. We all smoked in silence after the meal.

Maria ate quietly with the women, hand to mouth, hand to mouth, her eyes watching, ever watching.

I experienced a twinge of pain in my chest. I loathed bringing her into danger. Especially this particular danger. We were used to being chased.

Even by other lanun. But this felt like another level altogether. Someone out there hated me enough to chase me around the islands.

I wanted to keep Mari safe. I remembered the vow I'd made with her. She had come to me, looking for help. Now she was part of my life.

"You want to stay with the Orang Laut? Makcik will look after you," I said when we dispersed to our own rooms to sleep. Pakcik kept his wooden house swept clean, the roofs of fresh coconut fronds woven into a thick mat. Makcik provided clean plain sarongs for blankets. They had hung mosquito nets from the roof to shield us from the ever-present pest.

Maria's eyes were bright. "No. I am one of your men, I fight with you."

"This frigate chasing us … I am afraid it would hurt us," I whispered. "I feel someone has a grudge against me."

Maria gathered me into her arms. I leaned on her, breathing slowly. "I made a vow with you, remember."

"I remember. That's why I want to keep you safe."

I looked up into her eyes once more. I saw tears. This time, she was the eagle and I the helpless prey. She kissed me on the cheeks, and then on the lips. Her mouth tasted of mint and lemongrass. We were not onboard *Sri Matahari*. Close by, loud snores came from Pakcik's room. So we held each other tight instead, skin against skin, and wishing that the morning would bring better news. I held her, aching for deeper and more intimate touch.

WHEN WE FIRST MADE love, I was afraid. Like Maria, I had my secrets and scars to keep. Scars to keep hidden from the world. Maria had not questioned how I looked. I was not a typical man.

Once we were docked at a small port, off the coast of Melaka. It was small, because it only catered to the ships that plied in between the straits and in the archipelago. We had gotten closer, by then, and we desired to get closer. Halim had found us rooms in a local inn, just a small longhouse next to the jetty. The rooms were sparse: mats and watering basins. The mats were meant for sleep, a quick stay.

We had enough currency to have our own room. The men decided to sleep on *Sri Matahari*. Halim made the excuse that someone had to keep an eye on the perahu. There were thieves lurking everywhere.

So we both stared at one another, suddenly alone in our own room. I was fearful of what she would find out.

Maria drew me close and kissed me all over. Her scent was intoxicating. Awkwardly, not daring to breath, I removed my clothing slowly. When I stood before her naked, her eyes widened. But not in fear.

"Why, you are built like me," she gasped and smiled.

"Yes," I said and my face burned.

"There is no shame in that," Maria said.

"I am . . . not what you'd expected," I said quickly. Maria simply removed her tunic and pants. She was beautiful. A white moth began to dance around her, drawn to the light and her warmth. She giggled.

"There are people who are born in the wrong bodies. I was raised to accept people of all sorts," Maria said, pulling me to her. This close, with bare skin against bare skin, I could feel her heat and inhale her inner scent. She was sweet and salty like the sea around us.

I tentatively placed my hand on her bare breast and she shivered. I could see her nipples standing proud.

"I love and want you for who you are," Maria breathed next to my ear and kissed my neck. She began to move down, planting kisses along my body. Her lips were gentle, petal-soft. Her fingers tenderly caressed the scars, reminders of unpleasant encounters. They crisscrossed my stomach and thighs. In turn, I too saw marks on Maria's brown skin. Bibik used the rattan cane.

"Let's enjoy our night," she continued softly, leading me down to the mat.

AS A GESTURE OF gratitude, I gave Pakcik some of the brocade and a bottle of the Madeira. He once again asked me to stay. He was willing to shelter us as long as it took. He too had felt the danger. But I had men to feed, and a frigate to flee from.

"Be careful," Pakcik said, his voice sad now. "Sail with caution, just as the anglerfish lights its own way in the darkness. Remember your father's teachings. Listen to your own gut."

WE BARELY MADE IT out of the Tebrau Strait when the lookout spotted the frigate.

Maria, Halim and I exchanged glances. The hunter was back once more. This time, it would decide our fate.

Anger was a hot flame inside me. Why us? Why me? I was determined to keep *Sri Matahari* safe. As the perahu began her run, I stared at the frigate now looming closer. I heard that all-familiar sound, the whistle that was not a true whistle. The *Sri Matahari* rocked when the cannon grazed precariously closely to the rudder. Splinters broke. Maria gave an involuntary scream and she clamped a hand on her mouth, looking furious with herself.

"Damn!" I growled. First blood, but not of my own doing. I longed to return the favor. We did not have cannons. I was tempted to get one. "Abdullah!"

The helmsman redoubled his efforts. His brow was bleeding freely from a splinter's glancing blow. *Sri Matahari* gained speed. There was no time to dress Abdullah's wound.

The frigate and the perahu played a game of hiding and chasing. Out in the open sea without an island nor an islet in sight, the frigate was in its element. *Sri Matahari* was the loser. We were lanun. We were used to hunting in the sea and then seeking refuge in an island close by. Chase, hunt, hide. Now we were forced to keep running. Our supplies would run out. Pakcik had given us palm-wrapped tempeh and salted fish, with two handfuls of limes from his own fruit trees grown in wooden tubs. They were not enough. We needed drinkable water.

This hunt would wear us to the bone.

Another boom. The air shrilled. I swung around, about to yell as a cannonball splattered next to the bow, where Halim was crouched. Too close! He cursed the frigate in an obscure dialect. I believed he cast aspersions to the captain's parentage.

The frigate sailed close. I could see a man in a long black overcoat and brown boots, the fashion of the courts. He stood without fear. I knew without a doubt that this was no pale merchant pretending to be a sailor. Privateer. I had heard of this term being used to describe this type. He was no ordinary pirate. This one had been tasked to hunt prey.

He was yelling something. He was young. I could not gauge the physical appearance of orang asing as they seemed to age faster. Their skin worked differently from ours. I had a feeling he was my age, perhaps even younger. He had that kind of brashness only a young pirate would have—fearless, subject to no one. I was once like that. I thought I was invincible. Maria stiffened beside me.

"He's speaking Dutch," she hissed in my ear.

My hair instantly stood.

"He says you killed his brother. That ship we raided …"

"Was his brother's …"

Maria nodded. She squeezed my hand and did not let go. I felt her trembling now.

Blood feud.

He was out for my blood. Revenge.

Now it was pirate against pirate. His frigate, rigged to hunt and armed to fight more cumbersome vessels, was a worthy match for *Sri Matahari.* He could win this fight. He could kill all of us.

Sri Matahari flew once more, now desperately. The men were becoming tired. Halim looked more and more grim. He had wrapped clean cloth around Abdullah's head. Fortunately, it was a shallow cut and it had stopped bleeding by then.

The frigate was gaining ground.

I RECALLED THE TIME when we hunted the murderer of Maria's father. We had worked out a contract then—I to provide the ship, she to kill the man. That was when I first met her. Over revenge.

How Maria had blazed with incandescent fury, and how she looked at the murderer with such hatred and sorrow.

How she fought him with the ferocity of a she-harimau, sinking her blade into his chest. Staking it right into his heart.

Oh, how I loved that spirit in her, the fire.

WE HAD TO FIGHT differently. The orang asing fought with guns and cannons. We fought with our wits.

When the frigate drew alongside, *Sri Matahari* was dead in the water. The men lay on the wooden decks. I slumped next to Abdullah. Maria crumpled next to me. Halim lay further up, close to the bow where he fell. Victims of the cannons. Worn down by the chase. We had given up.

Our eyes met. He nodded slowly.

Let them think we have lost this battle.

I thought of ibu, of her patient pounding of the mortar in the kitchen. The taste of sambal tumis in my mouth, the fiery redness.

I thought of Maria. Oh, gentle sweet Maria. Mari. My saint.

My saint.

The frigate's men threw boarding ropes over. They climbed down. They stank of stale sweat and alcohol. The captain must have pushed them hard. What a pathetic crew. I squashed the sudden burst of sympathy.

Maria twitched.

A gleam of silver under her chest.

I began counting my heartbeats under my breath.

Feet thudded loudly as they boarded *Sri Matahari*. They wore ragged boots, some with their toes showing. I heard their laughter, their strange polyglot of English and Dutch with Portuguese thrown in. So they had a mixed crew of men from various western powers. What harsh languages. They seemed to growl from the throat. They moved about, examining the perahu. I was sure they made fun of the ship with their mocking laughter. They always thought their frigates and galleons were stronger than ours.

I glimpsed a new pair of boots this time. They stood out. The captain wore brown boots. They looked much sturdier than the rest. Better leather and workmanship.

"Now!" I snarled.

We leapt forth, screaming like enraged spirits.

Krises and daggers slit throats. The frigate's sailors toppled over, one by one.

My eyes met the furious eyes of the frigate's captain. He had such strange blue eyes. I shouted something and he responded in kind. Everything seemed to move slowly. My hands gripped the handle of my dao and I flew towards him—the captain's eyes widened when the dao pierced his chest. Something sharp hit my right shoulder. Belatedly, I found out it was the tip of his saber. The sharpness turned into fire.

I gritted my teeth and jammed the dao deeper. I had hit his heart. Blood flowed from his open mouth.

"You. Killed. Brother."

He spat out the pidgin words as if they were bullets.

I stared into his blue eyes. The light in them was fading.

"I am lanun," I said calmly. "This is my sea."

The captain died with his eyes shedding tears.

"You killed him," Maria said as if from a distance. "Neo . . ."

"I killed him for you," I said, or thought I said. No words seemed to come out. My ears seemed stuffed with wax. My shoulder felt as if it was being burnt by fire.

"You are hurt! Halim!" Maria was saying. Her mouth was moving. I could no longer hear words. I was falling into a black cocoon of silence.

"That was foolhardy of you," Halim said. He was the ship's physician. His family were bonesetters and herbalists. He was skilled with wounds and setting bones. He was the one foraging medicinal plants. "But . . . the tip did not enter deeper muscle. You will heal in time."

I would have yet another scar. I nodded numbly. Maria lifted a coconut husk filled with diluted lime-infused water to my lips. I sipped gratefully. The sourness invigorated me. Maria kept a small basket of calamansi limes on board.

We left the frigate alone this time. As an act of courtesy, we wrapped the captain and the men in cloth and lay them out in a neat row. Let the elements take them.

We took nothing. This hunt was not even worth the effort. There was nothing to trade. Nothing.

Sri Matahari limped back to Selat Tebrau. Pakcik found his best healer to treat me and some of the men who had been hurt. No further question was asked. I suddenly felt extremely tired. I sighed with relief when the poultice cooled the inflamed shoulder wound. The healer bandaged it tightly.

"You said you killed him for me," Maria said while I rested on clean mats. My shoulder throbbed and would hurt in the future. I was sure of it.

"You hate the Dutch," I said.

Maria opened her mouth as if in surprise. Then, she impulsively hugged me, causing me to yelp in pain. She apologized profusely and kissed me again and again. "Oh, you sentimental fool . . ."

"Only a fool for you," I said weakly.

She blushed immediately, catching herself before speaking again.

"Halim said no more raids until the next season." Maria arranged the sheets into a rectangle. She gently eased me down to the makeshift pillow.

"*Sri Matahari* needs repairs. Pakcik had his sons start work on them."

"The cannonballs!" I said. I now dreaded the sound.

"I hate them too. Shhh, time to rest. You know how tetchy Halim gets when his advice gets ignored..."

The healer had concocted an herbal brew. It was bitter with a sour aftertaste, but drinking it helped with the pain. It took the edge away and turned it into a dull ache. It also made me extremely drowsy.

"Sleep. You need to rest."

"I know."

The last thing I saw before I dropped into a deep sleep was Maria sewing torn clothing with needle and thread, her body's reassuring warmth next to me.

When I woke up again in the middle of the night, Maria was curled up beside me, her body spooning mine. My shoulder had gone pleasantly numb. I closed my eyes again and slept.

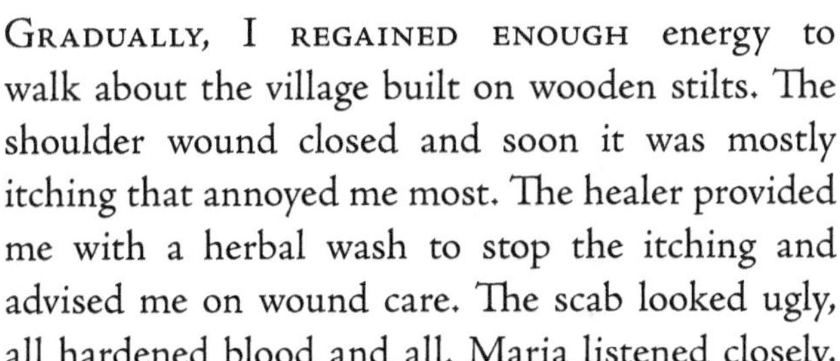

GRADUALLY, I REGAINED ENOUGH energy to walk about the village built on wooden stilts. The shoulder wound closed and soon it was mostly itching that annoyed me most. The healer provided me with a herbal wash to stop the itching and advised me on wound care. The scab looked ugly, all hardened blood and all. Maria listened closely, noting down the instructions. Her mind was a sponge. It kept everything.

Pakcik, Halim and Pakcik's sons were working on *Sri Matahari,* sealing any crack they could find and replacing the broken wood with resilient planks made from the local gelam trees. They also made new sails from the tree pulp. They were laughing and chatting about the upcoming layan festival. The villages would make ornate kites which they would fly to compete with one another.

I was eager to get back to the sea. Too long away from the sea and my body reacted with nervous tics. I began to pace.

"You look as if you want to sail right away," Maria giggled.

"I am restless," I confessed.

"You are always restless." Maria rested her head on my good shoulder. Her freshly-washed hair smelled of jasmine and coconut oil. She was most pleased with the baths—she would join the women for their morning baths in the shallows of the river. Some of the women gave her coconut oil.

"You say as if it's a bad thing."

"You need to learn when to rest and when to fight. You don't know when to stop."

"Now you sound like Halim during his lecturing moments."

We watched as the Orang Laut youth sailed their small perahu. They had colorful sails. In the distance, they looked like birds. They raced one another with glee and with sheer exultation of being free. The Orang Laut held sailing contests. Above them sea eagles spiraled. It was a mated pair calling out to one another. Close by, small raptors surfed the thermals.

"We will return to raiding in about one week," I said. Maria sighed dramatically.

"I thought we could stay for their kite festival, you know," she said. "I had fun making the kite with Makcik and her girls. Makcik thinks they will win the competition."

I looked into her dark eyes. Something in me gave in and gave way.

"We can stay," I said finally. "I just have to tell Halim the good news."

Then I held Maria close and we listened to the shouts of the young racers echoing in the breeze. The sails were butterfly wings.

MAKCIK AND HER GIRL did win the kite fighting competition after all.

After the kite festival, we stayed a bit longer as Pakcik and Halim made sure we had enough supplies to last until we reached Sumatra, to the coastal villages of Madan. There was a kampong of lanun and their families who had made their home there. We would be welcomed there, as some of the folk were former shipmates and sailors.

I hoped we could do a bit of raiding and hunting. And some trade. The prospect of trade lightened my spirits. We still had the boxes of celadon, brocade and silk fabrics.

"No more hunting Dutch ships," Maria said, half-jokingly. "They are nothing but trouble."

"They are," I said. "But they are more frequent now . . . Pakcik says they are taking over Java."

Maria made a rude noise. She also said something else in Portuguese, but I did not understand what it was. The tone she used led me to believe that she still had hatred for the Dutch. Her eyes burned with the same fire I'd seen before. I couldn't blame her.

"Promise me you stick to silks and celadon," she said finally.

"And Madeira wine," I added.

"Silks and celadon," Maria said firmly. "Spices allowed."

"Spices definitely allowed."

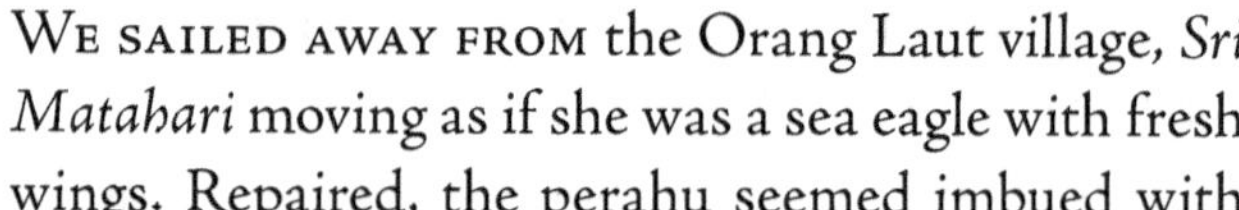

We sailed away from the Orang Laut village, *Sri Matahari* moving as if she was a sea eagle with fresh wings. Repaired, the perahu seemed imbued with new life.

I smiled. My shoulder throbbed a little. A reminder, always a reminder.

It was back to silks and celadon.

Trail of Silver

Chapter One

WHERE THE STRAITS INTERLACED each other with the confluences of currents and trade routes was the famed Golden Chersonese, a beacon of light, the center of all wealth and riches. Saints and bodhisattvas met there, allies in the inter-exchange of spirituality and learning. You would find your path there, they said. You would never hunger nor would you thirst. Bewitching creatures lurked in the Golden Chersonese, fantastic animals that populated your mind's bestiary. Beautiful birds of paradise with tails that flamed like the sun, dragons with large flickering tongues and poisonous saliva, and large cats that roared and founded a city.

From the lush jungles of the Khmer Lands to the crystal-clear waters of the Nusantara, the Golden Chersonese called out like the siren of the

Grecian myths. It lured many explorers, sailors of the sea and wind. It lured me.

Now I stood on the proud perahu, *Sri Matahari*. Sea salt coated my skin, sea wind curling through my hair. This late into the monsoon season, I had also shaved my hair close to the scalp. It was hot and humid; the torrential rains brought relief, but it also meant the ship stayed at port, unable to sail. No earnings for me and my men. Our pockets were emptier than usual. I glanced at the sky. It remained a dour grey, hinting of rain, but grudgingly holding back.

Beside me Maria adjusted her tanjak. She gazed into the distance, where the sea kissed the sky. I could spy some white sails, ships brave enough to carve through the water for the day. Fishermen, I thought. Perhaps we should fish too.

Maria's full name was Maria Fernandes, adopted by a Peranakan family as a servant, but found her freedom and revenge when she first met me. I was the captain of the perahu that found the man who killed her father. She in turn killed him with a blade plunged deep inside his chest.

And now she sailed with me.

Our relationship was close. Intimate. She lay beside me at night. Her lips were tender on my bare shoulders. The men left us alone, aware of our need for privacy and respectful as well. We were lanun after all, unbound by the rules and laws of normal men.

She called me Neo. I had long discarded my given name. I called her Mari in private.

"We can't sail," Halim interrupted the silence with a soft cough. "The winds are unfavorable and there is a storm inbound."

He was right: the horizon had begun to darken ominously, a churning blackness. I felt a stifling oppression descend. It was as if air was being sucked away by some angry deity.

"Look," Maria pointed. "The cloud. It's moving fast."

I looked. It was long and serpentine, with distinctive features of beard and horns like Sambar deer. It was a cloud, but it also looked very much like a Naga. The Khmer folk called them Nak. I shook my head. It was a cloud. Clouds did not have horns and beards.

The Naga had a bright eye, golden sunlight piercing through the darkness. A corona surrounded its head. It was a big Naga, an adult.

Did they have adults or children?

No. It *was* a cloud. The eye was the sun, the corona its halo.

A shiver went down my spine, unbidden. As a child, I had heard stories. Myths. Legends. Most were children's tales. Some were true, hidden in layers and parables. Of course, the Nagas were always creatures from the myths. The elders laughed and said that they were around, just that we needed the luck to see them out and about.

My skin crawled. There was a Naga in the sky. No, it was a cloud. My mind insisted it was a cloud.

I could not help but think that things were afoot.

THE STORM HIT US later in the afternoon, close to evening. It was fortunate that we had done our fishing early. As we grilled ikan kuning and roti from our leftover flour over the fire, glad for the shelter, the rain poured down like torrential sheets of water. It pounded on the corrugated iron roofs, it rattled the windows of the makeshift huts, it roared. Rivulets started to form outside our hut. The water flowed into the sea and kept on flowing. It seemed the rain would never stop.

It would rain until the next morning. Halim had the foresight to cover *Sri Matahari* with oil-cloth and keep her hull off the sand. Now she weathered the rain just as she had weathered it for a long time.

Maria and Halim made the roti out of the flour and water, kneading and shaping it into flat circles. I watched their deft hands move, slap the roti on the fire, and go on to make more, while lifting the cooked ones with a stick. Eaten with freshly grilled fish, the slightly crispy roti was heaven. To top off the meal, Halim had made hot soup of "everything," things he had scrounged, foraged and picked up from the markets. Lemongrass was boiled with white clams, bits of fish parts, root vegetables and a handful of white peppers, lashed with fermented fish sauce. It was ideal for the sudden dip of temperature. Hot, peppery and salty with a hint of sour.

We drank the soup from dried coconut shells using our fingers to pick out the shells and fish tails. The men flicked the clam shells onto the mat, eating enthusiastically. Even Maria was tucking in with gusto. She was innovative too, foraging for latok and ripe mangos. She was the one advising everyone to eat more fruits and vegetables, much to Halim's amusement.

When the meal was eaten, the husks cleared and washed, we all retreated to our respective corners. Oil lamps were lit, establishing warmth and privacy. Maria curled up beside me, warm and smelling of coconut oil and the finest of jasmine.

We did not speak for a while, content from the meal. The rain continued. Our world became our breathing, the sound of the rain and our heartbeat.

"Are Nagas real?" Maria snuggled closer.

I caressed her hair, enjoying her scent. "Some say they are myths."

"The cloud looked so real," Maria sighed. "I remember Bibik telling us about dragons too. Chinese dragons which they embroider on their kebayas. I saw mostly phoenixes. Dragons are real to the Peranakan."

"They usually mean good things," I said. The shiver was back, the hint of something in the air.

As a captain of a ship, I was used to these twitches. Like an extra sense.

"There is a festival in the Khmer Lands where a mysterious Naga is known to throw fireballs from a river. I wish I could see it one day." Maria smiled at me.

"Maybe one day." I kissed her head. "One day, Mari."

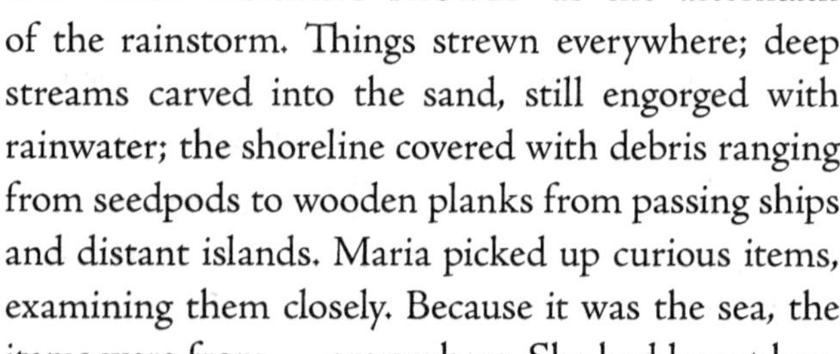

THE NEXT MORNING SHOWED us the aftermath of the rainstorm. Things strewn everywhere; deep streams carved into the sand, still engorged with rainwater; the shoreline covered with debris ranging from seedpods to wooden planks from passing ships and distant islands. Maria picked up curious items, examining them closely. Because it was the sea, the items were from . . . everywhere. She had learnt how to utilize the items she had found. Reusable baskets. Coconut husks. Driftwood she insisted was useful. Even pretty stones. She had collected a basketful of stones with holes in them.

Sri Matahari had escaped unscathed from the rainstorm. Halim and I breathed a sigh of relief. We could not tolerate a waterlogged boat or afford expensive repairs. Halim and Abdullah generally handled the basic repairs, at least. As the men rushed to check the hull for any damage and scrub the deck, I surveyed the scene with satisfaction and pride. We would survive and thrive another season.

"Do we sail today?" Halim asked. He was

eager to get back to the sea. We were all eager to get back to the sea.

I felt the wind whisper in my ear, the tug of longing *and* promise in my veins. "Yes," I said. "Let's sail."

Halim hurried off, yelling instructions and commands to the men. Abdullah, our helmsman, leapt straight onto the perahu. The prospect of a hunt fired our blood. I tightened my tanjak and my silk trousers, patting my dao tucked in my belt. One or two more successive raids—and I could visit ibu. Our luck would change. We would have successful raids.

Rest for a while. Take Maria to see ibu. Cook for ibu. Travel to the Khmer Lands . . .

Rest. Truly rest and breathe.

"Neo."

It was Maria's voice. But so unlike her usual cheerfulness.

"I want you to see this." She nudged me gently. She was cupping something in her hands.

I could see through the egg. It swam in its own amber light, a tiny serpentine form held suspended by fluids and something else. I thought I saw the beginnings of horns and a vestigial beard.

"A mermaid's purse," I said curtly. "A shark egg. They look like that when they are unhatched."

What surprised me were Maria's tears. They gleamed bright in the sun. "Naga egg. They are real, Neo. Nagas are real."

"Mari, it's a shark egg. The baby shark looks like a lizard."

"Neo, it is a Naga egg. I can feel it." Her tone told me not to argue further with her. She could be stubborn like that. I let it go. I personally thought she was behaving like a child.

No such thing as Nagas.

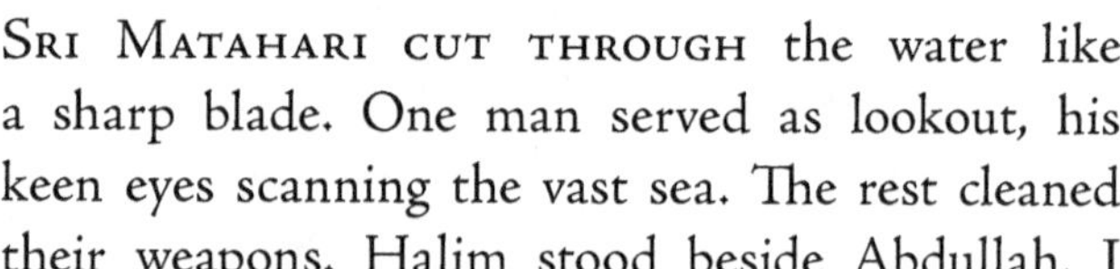

SRI MATAHARI CUT THROUGH the water like a sharp blade. One man served as lookout, his keen eyes scanning the vast sea. The rest cleaned their weapons. Halim stood beside Abdullah. I found myself standing alone. The men knew when Kapitan wanted space.

I watched Maria as she polished her dagger. The egg was nestled in a cloth pouch close to her chest. I attempted to convince her it was a shark egg once more. Shark eggs were common on the shores. The sharks laid them in the sea. Sometimes, the eggs detached from the rocks and floated elsewhere. She could not listen to me. She would not listen to me. She was convinced the egg was a Naga egg. This was why I was drawn to her: her stubborn, rebellious, indomitable spirit.

Something was coming.

I felt it in my bones.

I wasn't sure if we were ready to face it.

Chapter Two

MY PREDICTION BECAME TRUE: we raided our first ship after the rainstorm. It was a lone Javanese perahu, similar in build to *Sri Matahari*, laden with chests containing songket fabric, gaharu wood and pepper. We left the crew alive, but their ship foundered without its sail.

We could sell off the finely-made songket fabric and the wood, because they fetched huge prices in the marketplaces. Silk, songket and brocade. They were always welcomed by lanun and merchant alike. The pepper we would keep, because spices were still important currency. It was high-quality pepper too, so I was secretly pleased with our raid.

At one of the small towns, I bought an amber rosary for Maria. The gift made her giggle like a little girl. Her old Bibik mistress was harsh and was never generous. Gifts were often conditional. She was more generous when it came to the use of the cane. Maria held the rosary, admiring its beauty. She was still very Portuguese Kristang in her core.

Serani. Sometimes, I could see her praying quietly. Belief and faith was a solid light pillar within her.

After a brief sojourn and another short rainstorm, we sailed forth once more. Halim spotted larger prey: an Arabian dhow. It was a beautiful ship, elegant and built to race the wind. Perhaps I would have a dhow like it, but my heart was already given to *Sri Matahari*. The hunt yielded more riches than the Javanese perahu: besides bolts of silk, the chests bore gold, ivory and precious stones as bright as the stars in the sky.

The men were ecstatic. Halim danced an impromptu silat. Maria stared at the chests in disbelief. "This is the largest haul we have ever captured," she said. "Ah, Deus abençoe." I saw her fingers briefly touch her chest, where the egg was hidden. The *shark* egg, I thought.

I portioned out the profits to each of the men. They would retire well in the future, feed their families and children. We sold the bolts of silk off to a trusted dealer I knew. Kept two, so that we could make a decent kebaya for Maria and for ibu. For that special day.

One day.

That night, *Sri Matahari* rang with the songs of merriment. I permitted drink this time, an arak we had procured from a Dayak tribe after bartering a box of smokes. We sang, we laughed, we danced. When it was all over, we lay on the deck, staring up at the stars. I held Maria's hand while she dozed.

She wasn't used to the arak's strong intoxication and she got tipsy easily. My dreams were of dancing Nagas in a silver river, their snakelike forms surrounded by fireballs. Then one of the Nagas turned to face me and her eyes burned.

HALIM WAS THE FIRST to wake up, looking refreshed as if nothing had happened the night before. He prepared the fire, did the fishing and roused the men—still hung over—from their mats soon after by dousing them with cold water. Halim was my first mate, trusted above all, and my father's right-hand man a long time ago. He had sworn to my father that he would protect me and stay by my side. He taught me how to fight and defend myself—in some ways, he was my second father.

He served as my voice of reason too. His eyes were clear when he walked up to me, swathed in his plain brown sarong and tanjak.

"Profits like that," he said without preamble, "are a gift from Allah. They are miracles straight from His bosom. I would suggest some caution. Maybe our next hunt would be a failure, as most of the time they have been."

I knew Halim. I saw his body language. The tiny signs. The stiff shoulders. The straight back. The familiar posture he liked to take when he wanted to speak up about something. Halim had an uncanny sense like me.

"I don't put trust in signs and portents," he

continued, tugging at his tanjak with his right hand. I saw the scars on it. They were from his past. "I fear the wrath of Allah, of Tuhan instead."

He had seen the cloud formation. He was there.

"Put that fear in the men," I said. "I do not want them to become lazy and think that raids are easier from now."

He nodded and ambled off, gathering the men so that he could talk to them. I was certain that our third raid would be a failure. Luck was often fickle with lanun, generous one moment before turning cruel. The sea was like that too.

"What's wrong with Halim? He looks like he's bitten into a hot chili," Maria said. She combed her dark brown hair with her fingers. I loved how she looked, her hair golden in the sun. Halim, by now, was talking quickly, gesturing with his hands.

"He thinks we are just lucky, with our raids," I replied. The morning sun seemed to blaze brighter. My skin felt the heat. Such was the monsoon season. Would there be wind later? Already the air felt as if it was sucked away.

"We are lucky," Maria said.

"Not because of the shark egg . . . whatever egg," I said half-teasingly. Maria pouted. She did not find it amusing.

"Fine. It is a *shark* egg then. I am not a child. I know how shark eggs look. I grew up next to the sea too." She sounded angry now. Her eyes shone.

She gently lifted the egg out from its cloth pouch. I shuddered instantly. The moment I looked at it, the more it wasn't a shark egg. It was oval, the shape of a hen's egg, but as big as Maria's open palm. It didn't seem to have a shell like a bird's or a monitor lizard's; perhaps it was just transparent, like sea glass. The tiny form was all curled up and I could swear I could see a tiny pulsating heart. It began to twitch as if it had sensed our presence. The heart beat with its own rhythm. Thum-thum, thum-thum. Maria seemed transfixed by the heart.

I touched her shoulder and she looked up, startled. She smiled sheepishly, laced with a kind of loss.

"Maybe it's a baby shark after all," Maria said, her voice sad. "I was a child. I deluded myself into thinking it was some Naga's egg."

"We are allowed to make mistakes," I said gently. I felt bad for making fun of her. I decided that I would make it up to her later.

Maria inhaled deeply. "Let me release it in the water." She strode to the shoreline, dipping her toes into the shallows. Then she waded into the arched roots of the mangroves. I lost sight of her. She was gone for a while. All I could hear was the splash of the waves and the rustle of the mangrove leaves as they moved in the slight breeze.

When she came back, there were tears on her face. Yet, she was smiling. Smiling with tears rolling down her cheeks.

"Let's go." She took my hand and I lost myself in her liquid eyes.

OUR NEXT TARGET WAS a schooner. We chased the small schooner for hours. It was a game of hide and chase, weaving in and out of the inlets and small islands. The captain of the Melakan ship was as wily as me, willing to toy with me and my men. Yet, as the hunt went late into the late evening, when the light faded, the Melakan ship grew weaker and slowed down so much so we could sidle up beside it. I remembered the defiant eyes of the captain as he knelt on the deck of his ship. "Kill me," he seemed to challenge me. I spared his life. I didn't believe in killing without cause. The schooner was left adrift after we had taken all the chests and crates from its hold.

More silks, exquisite ceramics from the famed lands of the Middle Kingdom, and spices. Nutmeg this time. What riches. The men were happy. I was pleased. Then, I recalled Halim's words—and Maria . . .

"Fujianese gingbai." I traced a wondering finger on the curve of a beautiful green vase. It was smooth to the touch. Halim checked the rest in the crate, muttering at the amount of rough bedding they used to protect the fragile vases. Dried leaves and coconut husks littered the deck.

Maria squirreled some away for later use.

Hearts full, we sheltered at one of the inlets.

No storms that evening. The sky still crackled with heat lightning, the clouds glowing eerily with the flicker of green light. I thought I spied serpentine shapes swirling about the fast-flowing clouds. Clouds, I told myself. Just clouds. Halim made his "everything" soup again; it was thinner this time, with mostly clams, seaweed and salt from his personal stash. Maria supplemented with more ikan kuning she caught. The soup tasted fishy, but the men drank as if it was soup from heaven, made by the best cooks found in the Nusantara. I picked at the grilled fish, staring fitfully at the sky. The soup tasted bland to me. I was not that hungry. Maria remained strangely silent, seemingly lost in her own world. She had fought well earlier, showing no fear. Was she still angry with me for making her put the shark egg back into the sea?

Night in the inlet was quiet. There was the sounds of insects and the occasional rustle of a larger animal moving through the mangroves. A wild boar, perhaps, foraging for food. It certainly sounded like one with all the snuffling and snorting. We were safe on board *Sri Matahari*, who had her own song of creaks and murmurs. A cluster of fireflies lit up the small tree next to the ship. Maria's face bore an expression of wonder: wide eyes, childlike. I watched the fireflies too. They had been part of my childhood. Maria reached out with her hand to touch one of the fireflies. It alighted on her open palm.

I confess my sleep was uncomfortable. The air grew stifling once more, the harbinger of a huge storm. Persistent warmth pressed on my skin. As I sat up, Maria still asleep next to me, I realized the land was grown silent. No insect sounds. No wild boar. Nothing. Even the waves had gone quiet.

Maria stirred. I patted her head, reassuring her.

The sky continued to roil with eldritch light. It would be a big storm, even bigger than the one we had encountered a week ago. I couldn't breathe. My senses screamed at me to get away from the inlet. Now. Now. Now.

I found myself scrambling to my feet, shaking. A dark finger slowly reached down from the heavens.

Chapter Three

WATERSPOUT!

As lanun and people who lived by the sea, we were all familiar with all manners of weather conditions. The winds. How the clouds moved. The waves. The waterspouts. The columns of fast-spinning water were dangerous. I had seen how they had easily destroyed villages by ripping the roofs off huts and shelters. Some waterspouts faded away even before gaining enough strength. Some would grow and grow until they spun out of control. A waterspout went through the island I lived on. We remembered houses destroyed by its sheer ferocity.

The tip of the dark finger touched the surface of the sea. It seemed to caress the waves, tickling them the way people would treat a favorite pet. It also began to broaden, becoming bigger and bigger.

I glanced over to Maria, to the rest of the ship. They all slept.

It would pass, I thought.

As if it had heard me, the waterspout turned direction and headed towards the inlet . . . towards us.

My heart sank. I shuddered.

I reached down to shake Maria awake. As she sat up, looking annoyed, I ran over to wake Halim.

"Waterspout," I said. "It's going to hit us."

The men woke up then and *Sri Matahari* erupted into a frenzy. We removed the mooring, pulled the rigging and pushed the perahu into the water. I yelled at the men to raise the sail. There was almost no wind. *Sri Matahari* was grounded, unable to move.

Maria grabbed my arm. She was frightened. With us, she had seen waterspouts before. But she was now terrified. This one seemed different.

"Go help Halim," I said, and she hurried off to assist my first mate. They were struggling with the sail.

Sri Matahari finally moved, grudgingly. She felt as if we were dragging her through thick mangrove mud. Finally, the sail caught the wind and the ship's speed changed. Even then, the waterspout drew ever closer. It was moving with intent.

"Faster," I shouted. I could hear it now. The howling and the hissing. It really sounded like a Naga roaring. All my senses were yelling at me to flee. Jump off the ship, swim away. Anything.

The sail billowed forward and we all fell as *Sri Matahari* leapt forward. She was running now. I hung onto the rope. We were being chased. *Sri*

Matahari was now prey. I was used to being hunted. Such was the life of a lanun. But . . . this was different. I was silently praying the waterspout would dissipate, as waterspouts tend to, after a while. The waterspout only gained more strength and speed, growing darker and larger. We could not outrun a waterspout.

"Brace, hold onto something!" I screamed frantically, grabbing Maria and holding onto her tightly. *Don't let go, Mari.* The hissing and the howling was upon us. I could never forget the sound. I caught a glimpse of sun-bright baleful eyes.

Then the waterspout hit us.

FACES SPUN BEFORE ME, mouths open, screaming. I was flying through the air. Maria never let go of me, her hand so tight the pain became a focal point.

"Mari!" I shouted.

The wind ripped my voice away.

We might die.

We will die.

We are going to die.

I heard wood being ripped apart, felt debris pelt my face and body. They stung like insect bites. Then, sharper bites, as larger wood pieces struck. My beautiful *Sri Matahari* was dying.

Maria.

Her grip loosened. I saw her receding, yanked away, her mouth open as if she was shouting my name.

Maria!

Mari!

My saint. My bodhisattva.

I am going to lose her.

I fought the wind, raging, screaming curses. A huge plank, a piece of *Sri Matahari*, slammed into me. Darkness was a blessed reprieve.

IBU STROKED MY FACE with a cool hand. I had a high fever. I often had high fevers when I was a child. The healers always said I had too much fire in me. Her fingers were cool, tender, against my feverish skin. Somewhere, somehow, I could smell spices. Cooking spices. Kari powder, freshly ground. Crushed coriander, with hands. Someone was making kari. I could hear laughter, soft chatter. Was I in ibu's kitchen?

Ice-cold water splashed on my face. I cried out. That was uncharacteristic of ibu. My father, then? *Is he there too?*

Then the cold water filled my nose and I began to choke.

I was drowning.

THE FIRST THING I saw, up close, was sand. River sand, I groggily recalled. My head hurt. My nose hurt. Tiny pebbles were digging into it.

I pushed myself up. I was lying face down.

Mari.

Fear shot through me. Where was I? It was a river bank I was lying on. Not one I was familiar with. Jungle rose behind and around me. The heat was unbearable. Oppressive. To my relief, I spotted *Sri Matahari* close by, the figures of the men rising up from the river bank, their expressions of shock and surprise. They patted their bodies and limbs, loudly exclaiming their sentiments. Halim was already up on his feet and stood, hands on hips, his face unreadable. He sported a small cut on his right cheek.

Mari.

Maria!

Frantically, I began searching for her. My heart beat hard within my chest. Tears burned hot in my eyes. I wanted . . .

"I found her," Abdullah cried. He had a shallow cut on his forehead, but otherwise looked unscathed. Most of the men had bruises and cuts.

Maria was being supported by Halim as she carefully rose to her feet. I quickly held her, glad that she had no visible wounds. A dull ache reminded me that I did receive bruises on my ribs. I would be sore for a while.

"Where are we?" Maria whispered.

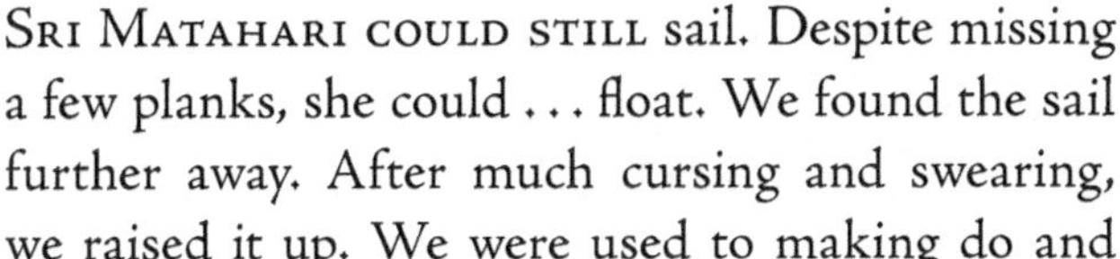

Sri Matahari could still sail. Despite missing a few planks, she could . . . float. We found the sail further away. After much cursing and swearing, we raised it up. We were used to making do and making what we could find—even in this strange land.

"I have never seen fishes like these before," Halim, ever the cook, said. "Perhaps inland. There are catfish. Also freshwater prawns. We can survive."

"We are inland and I don't recognize this place. Not Melaka, definitely," I said. "And it's definitely warmer here." The heat clung to our skin like wet cloth. It was hotter than Melaka.

The jungle steamed around us, thick and lush, like some green wall. I heard weird sounds. Animal calls. Something huge trumpeted nearby, echoed by similar sounds.

"Gajah," Halim said. "That's gajah. A whole herd of them."

Maria stared at the river. It flowed green and fast. "This river leads to a larger one."

"How can you tell?" I said.

She didn't answer me. Instead, she began to walk along the riverbank.

"We are not in the archipelago anymore," I said, watching Maria with concern. She had grown oddly quiet. Did the fall hurt her in any way? "That's for sure."

"I don't think waterspouts are able to transport people to other places . . ." Halim shook his head. "Strong winds, perhaps. But not waterspouts."

I sank to my haunches, running my fingers through the river sand. "Not seawater."

"Kapitan!" Khalid came running over. "You need to see this."

Khalid was our expert climber and rigger. He had apparently climbed one of the tall trees. I followed him, climbing slower. The bark was rough and black ants, bigger than the ones I'd seen, teemed on some of the branches. When we reached a certain height, Khalid simply pointed.

A yellow stupa rose in the misty distance. It reminded me of the temple at Borobudur. More small stupas stood around it—companion temples. They looked almost golden in the sun.

WE PUSHED SRI MATAHARI into the water, Halim checking every minute for leaks. We had managed to patch whatever hole or crack we could find with mud and clay. The men found a deposit of white clay close to the riverbank and we quickly got to work, covering the gaps with handfuls of clay. I worried that the white clay might not work and *Sri Matahari* would sink.

The perahu still creaked alarmingly. Sailing upstream would be a fight. So Halim and I agreed we would go with the current and see where it would bring us. We were still in possession of our weapons; we could protect ourselves.

Maria. My Mari.

She had her dagger in her belt. Her eyes were clear now. As *Sri Matahari* picked up speed, she walked to my side. I could feel her body's warmth.

She smelled of coconut oil and the sun, all the goodness in the world. I wanted to hold her forever.

"I haven't seen so much jungle before," she commented as the landscape flowed past in a continuous curtain of green. Birds flapped away from trees in flocks. I spied the occasional flash of bright blue—kingfishers. Large buaya sunned themselves on the riverbank, their toothy mouths wide open, their scaly bodies almost blending in with the mud. They looked larger than the ones I had seen.

The river seemed to widen and I saw columns of smoke. Cooking fires. That would mean villages. My heart pounded, half with excitement and half with fear. All my life I wanted adventure. To explore, to see the world . . .

Now I had the chance.

Dark-haired and brown-skinned children waved at us while they bathed in the shallows of the river. Their laughter was infectious, making me smile. Surely there were traders like us here. Feeling more confident, I stood at the helm of my ship, hand on my dao. I was ready for anything.

Chapter Four

"I BELIEVE WE ARE now in the lands above the Golden Chersonese," I said to the men. Their eyes were sober with absolute belief.

"The Khmer Lands," Halim said, nodding slowly.

It was not just the reaction from the men that unnerved me. It was also Maria's look of absolute trust. We were effectively marooned by a waterspout. How could that have happened?

How were we going to get home?

"We can ... trade," I added, a little lamely. "We can pretend we are merchants." I was grateful the goods were intact in the hold.

"Need to have cowrie shells and baked coins." Halim began searching through the box we'd kept for currencies. "At least, we have a small bagful of cowrie shells and some Chinese copper. That would last us for a week, at least."

Halim was ever cautious. He actually meant

that we did not have a lot to trade with and we could only survive for a few days.

As the skies began to darken, the splashes of orange and pink indicating sunset, we moored at a shaded alcove with overhanging banyan roots. It seemed cooler now, much to everyone's relief. Halim and Abdullah went fishing. Maria readied a small fire with the dried leaves and twigs she found. Two men stood on watch, ready for trouble.

I tried not to be lured by the serene landscape and the sound of the river. I had read about the warlike kings from these kingdoms, but I had also learnt about their arts and customs. Father used to tell us about his travels. These were the lands of the bodhisattvas.

Sunset. I worked out where we were, directionally. We were in the east of whatever land we were on.

After more rummaging through the stores, we found small clay lamps. With the cooking oil and leftover wick we could find, we lit them the moment the skies turned dark. Stars began to appear. Halim and Abdullah returned with two big catfish dangling from their makeshift bamboo poles. Gutted and cleaned, they smelled and tasted delicious over the fire, washed down with the clean river water.

Halim sat down for the night watch, hand on his kris. The night descended with a deep hush, interrupted only by insects and strange animal sounds. The hum of mosquitoes seemed oddly comforting in my ears. At least, these pests were everywhere.

Sleep was quick; I was so exhausted.

Someone was shaking me. I started awake, only to look into Maria's eyes. She was leaning close. Wordlessly, I followed her to the river's edge. The dark figure of Halim was a statue, solid and immovable.

Five fireballs were floating above the river. They glowed eerily reddish-orange.

They were not lanterns. Just balls of light.

Their light flickered on Maria's face. I saw wonder. Not for the first time, I felt the particular shiver run up my back. This was no simple trick of the eye. I remembered her telling me about the Khmer festival about Nagas and fireballs a while back. It seemed so long ago.

IN THE MORNING, WE did not speak of the fireballs we saw last night. Even Halim, who was there, had chosen to remain silent. I kept seeing the Naga and then the Naga's egg. And now we were in the Khmer Lands. It was not very hard to draw the connections.

My imagination was running wild. I hated it. I was the cold and rational kapitan of *Sri Matahari*. Not some superstitious fishwife seeing signs everywhere, fearful at first, then hopeful the next. Be careful what you wish for, ibu always said. I wanted to visit the Khmer Lands and now here I was, stuck in some unknown part of this strange region. I did not even have a map.

The men quietly went about their chores. It was surprisingly chilly at dawn and we found ourselves wrapped in whatever clothing we could find. A thin mist hovered above the river. Splashes were heard now and then. Halim made fire and breakfast. He found a petai tree and had harvested pods. Eating the green seeds raw together with grilled catfish and boiled river water, we had a simple meal.

The alcove was safe for bathing. So we all took the opportunity to wash up. Maria bathed, shielded by my spare sarong. The water was cold. I bathed after she was done. Tiny fish fry nibbled at my bare feet. So familiar, yet so foreign—I had seen similar scenes played out before, but in a saltwater mangrove or a secluded bay along the coast.

When I deemed we were ready, we pushed off once more.

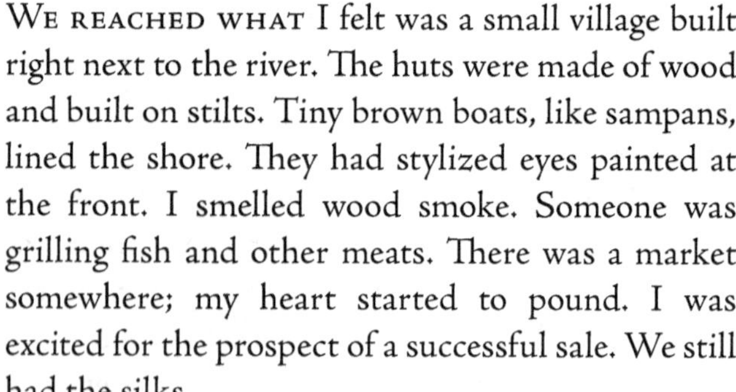

WE REACHED WHAT I felt was a small village built right next to the river. The huts were made of wood and built on stilts. Tiny brown boats, like sampans, lined the shore. They had stylized eyes painted at the front. I smelled wood smoke. Someone was grilling fish and other meats. There was a market somewhere; my heart started to pound. I was excited for the prospect of a successful sale. We still had the silks.

When we pulled in, a crowd of children

watched us with wide eyes. The boys were clothed in plain brown tunics; the girls had their chests covered with green cloth, leaving their stomachs bare. Their feet were bare, like the children of the Golden Chersonese. One or two had silver anklets. Halim tied the rope to a protruding rock. The children showed no panic or fear. One by one, we jumped out of *Sri Matahari*. Dressed like a man, Maria blended in with the rest of the crew.

It was a small village indeed, with a little market comprised of a few women selling produce on straw mats. An old lady was grilling small birds over a fire. Like the little girls, she wore brown clothing around her thin chest and a sarong. On her right shoulder, she had draped a brown shawl-like covering. Smiling kindly and using hand gestures, she offered us lodging in exchange for silk. Halim reluctantly agreed, considering our situation. We had nothing else to barter, except our loot. The woman's eyes were bright; she knew silk and she probably knew good silk, as she stroked the fabric lovingly with her fingers.

They make silk, I thought. Or, at least, they know people who make silk. I had heard about such skills in the Khmer Lands. They bred worms that made the silk.

The old lady patted her chest and said "Chan." I stared. She repeated the word again and I realized she was saying her name.

"Neo," I said in return, pointing to myself.

Chan prepared us food—bananas, grilled birds and white sticky rice. So they had rice too. She served them with a small clay dish containing a fishy-smelling brown liquid. It smelled, somewhat, like sambal belachan: pungent and redolent of the sea. It was fermented fish sauce, something similar to that used by Halim in his cooking ventures. Chan gestured eating the rice with the liquid. Maria's nose wrinkled, but she ate quietly. Like us, the Khmer folk too ate with their hands. The sauce was salty but delicious with the hot rice and the grilled bird.

The old woman's lodging was simple, spartan, with only straw mats for flooring. Her humble hut was built on stilts next to the riverbank. The men were content to sleep onboard *Sri Matahari*. If Chan had opinions about both Maria and I, she kept them to herself. Chan reminded me of my mother: small, quiet and intelligent in her own way.

Early morning came with the sounds of roosters crowing and children laughing as they bathed in the river. My sleep had been deep and profound. Chan had already woken up and was preparing for another day at the market. She was plucking feathers off the sparrows and munias she had caught with her fishing net. I helped her. For a while, we sat in silence, removing the feathers with our bare hands.

When we were done, Chan made us breakfast. Small fried fish, more of the hot sticky rice and the fish sauce. Then, with more hand gestures and enthusiastic attempts at drawing in the sand, she gave us what I thought were directions to a bigger village linked to the city. "Ang Kor," Chan said, pointing at the circle in the sand. "Ang Kor."

Maria looked at the jumble of circles and lines. Her dark eyes were inscrutable.

"What if she's leading us to a trap?" Halim asked me later, when *Sri Matahari* was back in the water, following the current.

I shook my head. Halim, the voice of reason again. I could understand his concern. "I trust Chan. She seems very sincere."

"Ang Kor . . ." Halim mused. "I have heard stories."

"What kind?" I said. He travelled with my father in his youth. They had journeyed to lands much further than the Golden Chersonese. There were stories he had never told me about.

"Not the Khmer Lands, but close. Heard of the land of Chaiya? I have encountered Tai people. They remind me of Chan and her village."

"You never told me about this."

"You never asked. As for Ang Kor . . . just myths. Stories to tell children before they sleep at night. "

"They are real, Halim. Not stories," I said.

Halim's gaze had turned distant. Indeed, his adventures in the past were mysteries. He turned back to Abdullah who had been doing an admirable job steering the perahu, leaving the conversation hanging. What happened in Chaiya that made Halim unable to speak of it further?

We spent the rest of the journey in silence. Maria held my hand, squeezed it, before going to help with the rigging. The wind seemed to have grown stronger and the sail billowed full. *Sri Matahari* flew, enjoying the speed. I began seeing more boats now. Even larger ones, the size of *Sri Matahari*, and of builds I had not seen before. Some looked familiar. Some were differently made, with more masts and sails. I realized that they might be from the Middle Kingdom. I recalled seeing one or two docked at Melaka.

There were fishing boats close to these vessels. Some things don't change much. As *Sri Matahari* drew close to them, the fishermen and women waved.

"Look," Maria cried.

The stupas of temples rose in the distance, gleaming gold and solemn grey granite. They were surrounded by smaller dwellings: stone buildings and huts made of more humble material. The stone buildings ringed the temples. I could hear, very faintly, sounds and noises of people and moving carts. A civilization.

A city.

"Ang Kor..." I said.

Chapter Five

SRI MATAHARI JOINED THE fleets of ships anchored and docked, a tiny ship out of many. The sails were brilliant white under the scorching sun, feathers of some mythical bird, shimmering in the light. The water seemed to shine too, glistening silver, as fishing boats darted to and fro to bring in their catch. As we stepped onto the river bank, fishermen carried baskets filled with fish still frantically flapping their tails to women clad similarly like Chan and the women of the village.

If the city of Melaka was busy, Ang Kor was hectic with sheer activity. People from everywhere thronged the streets, the noise and crush of bodies so overwhelming that Maria gripped my hand and never let go. I could not recognize some of the clothing styles! There were even oxen with large spreading horns and all sorts of animals, ranging from small kuda from the Spice Islands with orange and brown coats, stamping their hooves as if they hated the crowds, to fidgety inquisitive macaques sat on their owners' shoulders. As we squeezed through the ever-moving rivers of people, women and men called out to entice buyers. All manners of goods were on show here. Ceramics, all kinds of fruits, bolts of cloth and even weapons were displayed openly.

We walked and walked, until we reached what seemed the end of the street. It widened to a broader thoroughfare, with a straight path to the big temple, guarded by two rearing serpents. Maria gasped. The serpents had broad faces topped with tapering horns; their mouths were rimmed with sharp teeth. As guardians, they were formidable, even terrifying. They also bore an uncanny resemblance to the Naga I had seen ... weeks? ago.

Nak. Naga.

Things seemed to come full circle.

"We seem to have come to the right place," I found myself saying aloud. Maria glanced at me, and I could see she was similarly affected. She had tears streaming down her cheeks.

THE TEMPLE WAS FILLED with devotees, the air thick with the fragrances of agarwood and sandalwood. My attention was immediately drawn to the giant stone statue of the Buddha, his right hand held with palm out and fingers pointing upwards. I was raised agnostic, but I respected all faiths. I bowed and Maria did the same. I could never forget the image of her, head bowed, hands held together, her profile glowing under the sunlight.

I never forgot how she came into my life.

"I prayed for peace," Mari whispered later. "For both of us."

HALIM GOT US LODGINGS at an inn. How he managed to find the payment, I didn't ask (or want to). It was a fairly large inn with decent clean rooms (wooden floors and dry mats). They even had cloth pillows filled with fragrant rice husks! Each room had their own large ceramic basin of fresh water for washing and bathing. The water drained back into the river. I marveled at their city building. It was far more developed than Melaka.

The men seemed uneasy and awkward with the lavish settings. Halim shrugged. He sat contentedly at the window of his room, blowing smoke rings with his cheroot. How he managed to find his smokes was also beyond me. I watched him sprinkle some brown ash on fine paper and roll it up. "Herbal," he said. "Local weeds." The smell of the smoke was faintly minty, like cooking peppermint: sweet and sharp. Familiar.

Maria's desire was to explore the city. I was more circumspect and cautious. We were, after all, in a foreign land. I had seen traders from the lands I came from—so merchants did travel to such places. Surely they knew the way back. I had no real knowledge of the Khmer Lands; my expertise was the Golden Chersonese. I should have paid more attention during lessons. Cikgu Ridwan's voice droned on and on, and all I wanted to do was sail on the small and swift perahu jong and feel the sea wind on my face. Such were the follies of youth. As I grew up and travelled the seas, I began to appreciate the lessons and what they had taught me. The influences of the various cultures and faiths, the intermingling and the exchange of ideas and ideals as they were dispersed, took root and then bore fruit. The fates of the Golden Chersonese and the Khmer Lands were interlinked. The more I walked around, I caught bits of Old Malay, Portuguese and Chinese in the pidgin trade tongue.

We retired early, overwhelmed by the sights and sounds of the city. The owner of the inn served us platters of sautéed meats with fresh vegetables and rice, before bowing and leaving us alone. He explained, through hand gestures, that it was a festival night and he had to go to the temple. As the night wore on, there was music, of pipes and drums being played, and singing, distant, as if coming from the temple. Even something like gamelan. The hypnotic rhythms seemed to move with the pulse of the river. Maria stood by the window of our room, looking out into the darkness. The inn was close to the river. Lights floated down it, like stars in the sky.

THE NEXT MORNING, THE innkeeper informed us as he served us hot rice and a thin sour tamarind soup that the city was celebrating their festival of the dead. The month was dedicated to remembering their ancestors and deceased family members. The festival would end on the fifteenth day—a full moon.

Nagas. Naks. Now a festival of the dead.

Halim looked pointedly at me. "Coincidence," I said, my tone curt. "We shouldn't put too much into signs."

We decided to explore more of the city, savoring the food and learning more about the culture. I saw similarities: the fruits were familiar to me, some of the meats I had encountered before. Yet, I also saw differences. Unlike the islands where I hailed from, this was a land where Buddhism had taken root and was the dominant religion. These folk were open and tolerant of people of all kinds and—indeed of different faiths. I swore I had seen Melakan traders in sarong and tanjak amicably mingling with merchants from the Middle Kingdom. They were sharing rice wine and riotous jokes over a table laden with delicacies of fish and roast chicken. It would seem that they spoke the pidgin trade tongue and used additional hand gestures for emphasis. I was determined to learn the pidgin as much as I could. Perhaps I could use this if I travelled to this land in the future . . .

If I could find a way back *and* survive in the first place.

Why was I brought here?

Halim, too, had noticed and heard the pidgin.

He smiled briefly and went on alone by himself to barter with a trader who laughed and greeted him like a long-lost brother. They exchanged smokes and began chatting.

Maria simply stared around, like a child in a wonderland. To her, Melaka was big. Ang Kor was immense, so much larger and busier. We had currency and coins now, thanks to Halim who had the foresight to sell the songket fabric. She went about, sampling food, touching bolts of cloth and admiring beautiful ceramics.

I tried using the pidgin. At first, it was awkward, but as the day became late afternoon, I grew more confident with the smattering of words and hand gestures.

We saw remnants of last night's celebrations—small palm-sized "boats" made of large bamboo and banana leaves washed up to the shore. They were filled with flower buds and candles, all looking totally soaked and limp.

"I asked for directions back to the Golden Chersonese," Halim said when we all gathered for the evening meal. The men had also returned with information. "There is a way back, but it takes a longer route."

"Then let's plan to return," I said. "We can sail back here again. It feels like a good place to trade."

Halim lit his smoke. "We shall see."

Chapter Six

THE NAGA DIPPED HER head down until her bright gemlike eyes met mine. I could smell her—redolent of spices and the sea. Her scales gleamed, ruby and emerald. I knew she could be kind and fierce. This time, she was fierce, a brewing thunderstorm threatening to overwhelm me.

"Where is my child?" She blew sea air into my face. Her voice was a gale, her serpentine body giant waves.

I stared at her ferocious eyes. They were twin suns. The irises were maelstroms, swirling erratically.

"I don't know where your child is."

"You lie!"

I stared at her, unable to speak, unable to answer.

I SAT UP FROM the mat bed, suddenly feeling lost. I did not know where I was. The walls were closing in. All I remembered were Naga eyes boring down into me. Frantic, I looked around, only to find Maria curled up next to me. Then the feeling eased and I felt more myself. The night was quiet, interspersed by the usual sounds of a city in slumber. The cries of babies, the coughs of men and women, and whispered conversations in the dark. The walls were thin, and privacy was a privilege. I could hear another pair from another building coupling. I could even hear the river.

A sleepy Maria drew me back to the mat bed. Her lips brushed my shoulders, my neck. Warmth spooled between my thighs, and I pulled her to me, to my lips. Our kiss became deep; we drank each other in.

"Mari . . ." I was drowning in her pleasure, our pleasure.

"Shhh . . ." Mari sighed, her breath now quick. I inhaled all her scents: jasmine, coconut and her special sweetness between her thighs.

We made love in the dark and our sighs joined the night sounds of Ang Kor.

RAISED VOICES WOKE US up. It was already morning, the sunlight streaming into the room. And warm too, so similar to the islands and the archipelago I was used to. The raised voices were not of fear, though, but of excitement. Maria clambered off the mat and went to the window, wrapping a sarong around her bare body. She gasped, as if delighted, and I joined her at her side.

People of the city were crowding the riverbank. They were dressed in all kinds of garments, but the chest wraps and pants were dominant. Monks in saffron robes had joined the crowd. I could hear distant music: the sound of drums, cymbals and more of the gamelan. There were certainly crossovers in terms of our literature and music. They were chanting. Halim had said it was either some kind of smot or puja for revered religious figures.

With a sudden hush, the spectators raised their joined palms to their forehead, bowing reverently. There was a flash of gold—and I gasped too, my fears forgotten at the sight of an astonishingly beautiful ship gliding down the river. At its prow was a dragon's head, a Naga's head, shining with gold and gems. The entire ship was shaped like a Naga, complete with tail. Men in fine gold silk livery stood on the deck, looking like royal guards. They bore spears and shields. I saw the rows of oars churning the water rhythmically. A silk-curtained pavilion shielded their very important passengers. The pavilion was coated with gold too. Next to the pavilion sat musicians playing instruments.

The dragon ship sailed down the jade-green water. It was accompanied by small ships, similarly gilded.

"That must be a king or a queen," Maria said. The spectators continued bowing until the last of the smaller ships had disappeared. Then, they simply dispersed. "I am reminded of the Srivijayan nobles I read about."

"Srivijaya held powerful sway in the Golden Chersonese and beyond," I said. "Temasek was under its rule. So was the rest of the archipelago, our Nusantara. I am not surprised its empire is vast. I hear Malay words in the pidgin tongue."

The thought of going home rose in my mind once more. We could go home. *We could go home.*

Maria went about washing her hair. She had steeped jasmine flowers she'd bought in a copper basin filled with clean water. She had fallen silent again.

THE KING AND HIS favorite consort were indeed in the city, having sailed from the capitol. They were here to present their offerings at the temple. What I gathered from Chheang, the innkeeper, was that the favorite consort had borne the king a healthy son and the offerings were their way of giving thanks. It seemed, at the birth of the prince, a royal Nak came down from heaven and flew over the palace. The Nak had bestowed, according to Chheang, power and luck to the prince. He would be the next in line—the Crown Prince. Such news warranted celebration. With the festival of the dead ending, it was an auspicious sign.

I stifled a shudder. *Why are Naks and Nagas appearing everywhere?*

No more signs.

That night, the sky was lit with floating lanterns. I knew them as sky lanterns, and they came from the Middle Kingdom. Their popularity seemed to have spread. With Maria and Halim, I watched the glowing lanterns ascend in the sky. They rose higher and higher, becoming dots. Maria remarked they looked like stars. There was singing and dancing in the streets, much drumming and the haunting music of the gamelan-like instrument. Maidens dressed in bright yellow silks danced. Children played with joyful shouts; they had colorful spinning tops and cloth balls. The festival had ended and the people celebrated the birth of a dragon prince. Life and death, intertwined.

"Where is my child?" she blew sea air into my face. Her voice was a gale, her serpentine body giant waves.

"I don't know where your child is . . ." I said.

The Naga dipped her head down until her bright gemlike eyes met mine. I could smell her—redolent of sandalwood incense, spices and the sea. Her scales gleamed, ruby and emerald. I knew she could be kind and fierce. Her storm eyes spun and spun like the children's tops.

"Where is my child?" she repeated. "You lie! I want my child back." Her eyes mesmerized me. She would strike me down where I stood.

"I don't know where your child is…" I repeated.

THE CELEBRATIONS WENT ON for a few days. The king and his favorite consort stayed in a private palace close to the temple, shielded from curious eyes. We watched the city folk bring their best produce in processions of yellow flowers, fruits, freshly slaughtered fowl and caught fish. Many of the tributes bore expensive gold foil. They were all extremely extravagant. Even a Sultan's birthday was not that elaborate. Many of the city folk collected the foil and flowers that had fallen off the tribute processions for good luck. Blessed, as they said, by the king and the Naga.

"Chrysanthemums," Maria said. "I love their fragrance."

Meanwhile, Halim got *Sri Matahari* ready for travel again. He had managed to find repairmen (again with what currency I didn't know). He smoked while he watched the men work all over the perahu, making sure they followed his instructions. He loved the ship as much as I did.

"There were a lot of fish swarming all over *Sri Matahari* this morning," he told me while we had our breakfast of sticky rice and minced spicy chicken meat. "Carp, even catfish. They were churning about. Probably a spawning of some sort and they were all eating the eggs. The men . . . they caught some of the fish. They were so delighted with the abundance. The fishermen too."

"I see," I said and chewed my food. The chicken

meat was wonderful with fresh raw vegetables. A harmonious combination.

"We caulked so many holes in the ship. But now we are seaworthy! Just follow the rivers and small streams and we will reach the sea." Halim sounded happy. His eyes shone. "The men miss their familiar hunting grounds, Kapitan."

"So do I," I replied. I put away the bowls. "We should get ready to set sail. Get enough supplies. Fresh water. Limes. I suspect we will be sailing for a while."

"I will inform the men," Halim said and got up from his seat. I nodded, looking for Maria. I saw her by the river, staring into the distance.

"We are going home soon," I said. She had been so distant, of late. She turned to face me, and her eyes were dark, haunted. "Mari, what is wrong?"

"Nothing. I am well. Going home . . ." she whispered softly. "I would like that."

I held her close, smelling the fragrances of jasmine and coconut oil.

"It would be safe here," she murmured.

Her sentence struck me as strange.

"Mari?"

Her brown face suddenly brightened, as if a veil had been lifted. The sun had emerged once more. My Mari had returned. "Let's go home!"

"I don't know where your child is . . ." I said.

The Naga dipped her head down until her

bright gemlike eyes met mine. I could smell her—redolent of spices and the sea. Her scales gleamed, ruby and emerald. I knew she could be kind and fierce. She was fierce now. She would kill me.

"Where is my child?" she repeated. "I want my child back."

"I do not have your child. I don't know where it is."

Liar, liar, liar.

The Naga reared back and I could have sworn the eyes dripped diamond tears. The air turned cold. There was ice on my breath.

"My child is gone," her voice sobbed, the tone of a mourning mother. "Come back, child. Come back to me."

Chapter Seven

THE STORM STRUCK THE city in the morning with ferocious wrath.

The rain pummeled it. We ended up retreating into the inn, all repairs and preparations halted. For hours, the rain fell and the streets became miniature rivers of brown water and mud.

"Must be the monsoon," Halim remarked and lit one of his herbal cigarettes. The men sighed and lounged like lost souls bereft of purpose. They hung about, looking listless. I was just glad we had enough to pay Chheang. Chheang, to his credit, had been generous and supportive, extending our stay without any compensation.

"You brought in business!" the innkeeper would say, in the pidgin port tongue. "Good, good!"

Maria kept staring out of the window, out into the river now blurry because of the heavy rain. All the fishing boats hid from the downpour. The merchant ships merely huddled and endured the onslaught.

THE DOWNPOUR SOON EASED and I later found Maria at the riverbank, next to *Sri Matahari's* dry dock. Halim had the perahu moved to dry land so that the repairs could be done. The ever-observant Halim had *Sri Matahari* covered with waxed cloth to keep her dry. He was pleased to learn treating cloth with melted beeswax from the helpful repairmen. I often saw them sat together, smoking their herbal cigarettes, talking with their hand signs. So, at the moment, *Sri Matahari* was dry and her bow kept off the ground.

Maria knelt by the shore, seemingly in a trance or a daze. She stirred the water idly with her hand. I walked closer, not wanting to disturb her. Her behavior had been odd these few days.

Something was also stirring beneath the water. It was long, like an eel, but the size of a feral cat. It seemed to have whiskers or barbells. And the shimmering of scales, gemlike, underwater. An enormous river carp? They were common in rivers. I must have made a noise because Maria looked up so quickly, so startled, that I even pulled back reflexively. She looked as if she had seen a ghost.

"Mari, are you well?" I said gently. "Are you hiding something from me?"

Maria opened her mouth and then closed it, her lips looking so kissable. Even at her most inscrutable, she was beautiful. "I . . . yes . . . no . . . I don't know."

Wavering doubt from the usually assured Maria. It was not like her at all. I grew worried. Because Maria would never lie. She was passionate about things, intensely so. But she wouldn't lie.

Would she?

Mari wouldn't. Growing up in her adopted home, under the Peranakan matriarch, lying would incur more punishment. Mari had told me that the Bibik would beat her (and the other adopted children) even for the smallest mistake. The scars left by the beatings were physical and had also etched deep in her and their minds. My Mari had grown up scared, afraid to lie. Lying would mean bad things would come their way. For a long time, she was unable to speak about it. Even now she looked as if she was about to burst out crying, so great was her fear.

"You don't know?" I asked, again gently.

"I don't know if I have truly done a good deed, or I have caused more trouble . . ." Maria brushed a wayward lock of hair away.

Unbidden the dream of the Nak rose. The damned Naga dream. Her spinning storm eyes. Her anger. Always her anger. A thin rain had started again, a dreary drizzle that promised more to come.

"Maria, what did you do?" I felt as if I stood in a cold shower of ice. Such was my feeling of terror it nearly overwhelmed speech.

"I . . . Remember the shark egg we argued about? The egg I insisted was a Naga's egg?"

"Oh, Mari..."

"I kept it... I didn't release it at all."

"Oh, Mari... why?"

Maria's face fell. "I don't know. I wanted... I wanted to protect it. So, I hid the egg in one of the holes I'd found on *Sri Matahari*."

"You hid the egg? Why did you not tell me?"

"Because I knew you would yell at me. Like you are doing now..."

I cursed myself for being such a horrible person. Maria shrank from me. It was Bibik all over again. "I am sorry. I am not yelling. I did tell you a long time ago we could talk things out..."

"You did, but... I didn't listen. The egg must have slipped out of the hole and hatched..."

"Hatched... Mari, did you know I have been having dreams of a Naga mother looking for her child?"

Maria placed a hand on her mouth. "Oh."

"And this weather could be her being really upset because she lost her child."

"See, you are yelling again," Maria said, her eyes afire. "And you should have told me the dreams."

"I am not yelling. I am sorry for not telling you about the dreams. I... I am just... worried and concerned and angry at you for hiding it from me. But I love you and I know you will do this sort of thing."

The fire abated. Maria actually smiled a little. A shy tentative smile.

"You know I will do this sort of thing?" she said softly.

"It's you. I fell in love with you because you are you." I could not help but also smile back. "You believe in your cause and you act on it."

"Oh." Maria placed her right hand on her mouth. Her cheeks were flushed.

"That eel-like fish in the water . . . is the Nak child," I suggested. She nodded.

"We should return the child to its mother."

"Her."

"Her?"

"It's a she. I don't know how I know but the Nak child is a dragoness."

"How can you . . .? Never mind." The whole situation had become bizarre, straight out from some myth, a child's story. No, it had become very real. No more myth.

But my heart had warmed at her blushing.

"Neo?" Maria touched my arm apologetically. My Mari. Ever so sweet in nature. "Are you angry with me?"

I looked deep into her eyes and shook my head. "Now the trick is to find her mother. The question is where do we start . . ."

HALIM PREDICTABLY LOST HIS temper when we told him the truth. He was mostly angry at Maria, who apologized so many times I'd lost count. Yet, he soon cooled down and simply looked weary and immensely disappointed with Maria. When Maria first joined the crew, Halim was the first to voice his concern. Maria was an unknown quantity. Maria would disrupt the ship. As she grew in skills and confidence, and earned the trust of the men, Halim grudgingly accepted her. More so when she became an intimate part of my life. The two found themselves working side by side in the early mornings, preparing food. Their cooking together soon became ship routine.

"The Naga could have killed us," he growled, stamping out his cigarette with some force. The embers danced frantically away. "Yet she didn't."

"It feels like she wants us to find her," Maria ventured bravely and fell silent when Halim glared at her. He had not forgiven her yet.

"But why?" Halim rubbed his jaw. "Kapitan, we are in danger."

"Let's find out if we are," I said grimly.

Chapter Eight

WE BID THE CITY of Ang Kor farewell, setting sail the moment sunlight burst through the clouds. A few of us looked back at the by-now familiar temple stupas and roofs wistfully. We had grown used to the creature comforts of food and bed and a roof above our heads. Chheang bade us farewell and hoped we would return again.

Yet this was not our true home. We were going back to the Golden Chersonese, following the map sketched out by Halim and Abdullah. The two had sat night after night, talking and poring over the parchment. I thought I somehow managed to make sense of the arrows, boxes and big dots made in black plant ink. Halim's drawing wasn't exactly the work of a trained cartographer and was rudimentary at best. The big dots were rest stops and smaller cities or villages. The boxes were marked unknown and *those* worried me. As a captain of a lanun ship, I knew danger when I saw it. We had encountered so many dangers. You would think we were used to it by now—a new day would bring a totally new danger, something we did not expect at all. This trip back home was going to be dangerous. There were just too many unknowns. We needed to play our cards carefully, use our supplies cautiously and not . . .

. . . offend a Naga mother who was convinced that she had lost her child. Her daughter.

How were we going to find her?

Both of them?

And the baby Nak . . . it was following the perahu like some loyal dog. I saw her head emerge from the water, just as *Sri Matahari* pulled away from Ang Kor's riverbank. She looked nothing like an eel, just a miniature version of the Naga, her mother, in the dream: frilled, gemlike eyes, and scales that shone white like the full moon. Did Nagas have types? Colorations? This one's scales were not like her mother's which were green-blue as the sea. Did they even have fathers? Or, because I had read somewhere, did they breed asexually, without the need of a mate, like some snakes or lizards? Were they even lizards?

And as *Sri Matahari* followed the flow of the river, the baby Nak paced alongside with us. With her presence, strange things were happening in and with the water. Fish swarmed about her, not biting her, but accompanying her like eager escorts. The area around her gleamed, the water crystal-clear, appearing as if it had been purified. She seemed to be making sure we had enough to eat. Even all kinds of fowl landed on the perahu.

Maria had named the baby Nak Mahsa, a Farsi word for "like the moon." I thought she was being whimsical, but I sensed she had forged a bond with Mahsa. I had spied her talking to the baby Nak and it . . . her . . . responding by dancing in the water, splashing with her fins.

Would the bond affect our own . . . bond?

"The water is sweet," Maria told me when we sat down to eat. "Like spring water, but only so much cleaner and purer." We seemed to be led to a grove of rambutan trees, the fruits all prickly and ripe. Fish, clean water and now fruits. We were not lacking in terms of food.

I nodded, because I did not know what to say. The whole thing with Mahsa was strange. My feelings about Maria and Mahsa were changing too. I felt as if I was about to lose Mari. I was going to lose her to a mythical creature.

How were we going to find Mahsa's mother?

What was she going to do to us when we finally found her?

WE PASSED BY VILLAGES where we briefly rested and replenished our supplies. At every stop, something miraculous happened to the village: they got a windfall of fruit enough to feed them for a month, the fishermen caught enough fish or they found a new source of fresh water. Mahsa ducked out of sight, remaining in the water, not daring to surface. I often saw Maria whispering to her. They seemed to have their own language composed of words and touches.

Where we had presently stopped, *Sri Matahari* seemingly glad to have a respite, the villagers found enough mulberry leaves to feed their silkworms. And out of season too, apparently, according to the village chief. We spoke with the pidgin trade tongue of words and hand signs. It seemed to be the language between merchants and villagers. It would boost the silk making for the next coming months and bring in more currency for the village. They gave us a gift of silk as a way of saying thank you.

Maria smiled with a look of contentment on her face, a glow to her skin. She was radiant. I shivered. I did not want to lose her. And I had to catch myself thinking like that, because the thoughts felt odd and grim. Why did I think I was going to lose her? Lose her to what?

Mahsa?

A little Naga?

Was I . . . jealous? That a little dragon had occupied the heart of my beloved?

The villagers were kind and generous enough to give us food and a night's lodging. That night, we watched the villagers sing and dance, around a lit bonfire, as fireflies pulsed their strange music on the trees and shrubs.

Halim smoked one of his cheroots and stared into the night. I could only hold Mari quietly. What else could I do?

"We found your daughter," I said in the dream. It began like the Naga dream: the Naga surfacing from, no, flying down from the sea of clouds. Her body gleamed and heaved like green waves.

The Naga regarded me, her eyes shining like diamonds. Yet the atmosphere remained cold, like stone. In fact, the water had turned into ice. I shivered, chilled to the bone.

"We found your daughter," I repeated. Even in the dream, I was unnerved. She felt as if she did not believe me, that I was some rank liar. Perhaps, in her eyes, I already was. "I speak the truth: we have found your daughter."

But I did lie to her.

I lied to her.

Then the Naga simply faded away, leaving behind a stream of stars. Or flower petals. Jasmine, I realized. I could smell them.

"Follow the stars," her thunder-like voice sighed.

Follow the stars.

That was the dictum of every seafarer, every captain. We followed the winds and we followed the directions of the stars. Follow the north star, it went. Follow it, because it is fixed. Bintang Utara. It was there and we followed it, no matter what. The night sky had its rhythms and the stars chased their positions. Yet the Bintang Utara remained constant.

"Find Bintang Utara," I told Abdullah the next morning. "Where is it in the sky?"

I scolded myself for not following back to the oldest of ways to sail. We should have followed the Bintang Utara right from the start.

The answer felt ever so close in my grasp.

WHILE WE MULLED OVER the directions, Mahsa grew rapidly. From the size of a house cat to the size and length of a perahu, she was no longer the small dragon we knew. She was as long as *Sri Matahari*, yet without the bulk of her formidable mother. Her horns seemed more distinct now, her features becoming more defined and . . . Naga-like. A cross between horse and reptile. Her scales remained moon-bright, shimmering faintly in the water, as she glided beside us, a mythical escort. She sang, a haunting high fluting voice that brought in birds and fishes.

Maria held me close every night, her breath soft against my neck. She slept soundly, without care. Without fear. She seemed to have found that center of joy or contentment. Nothing seemed to faze her, not even the foreign environment. I knew part of that strength came from the strengthening bond with Mahsa.

Abdullah found Bintang Utara with his keen eyes. It was a bright spot in the night sky, true north indeed. We should sail at night too, Halim suggested. Not to waste any time. I thought hard about it. Sailing at night could bring more dangers, especially on a river we were not familiar with. The land was treacherous enough. I did not want to further endanger the lives of my crew . . . and Mari.

WE SAT ANCHORED AT a secluded inlet in the evening, away from any village. The river had its—by now—familiar sounds of creaks, gurgles and the occasional loud splash. With the monsoon, there was also debris: tree trunks, branches and uprooted shrubs. Mahsa slipped around these obstacles easily, pushing them away for us with her body, a swish of her diaphanous fishtail, a swing of her horned head. She was enjoying herself.

She was a child, after all.

A dragon child, I reminded myself. An unpredictable dragon child.

Halim prepared the dinner meal of river crabs and some of the fruits given to us by the villagers. We all sat down to enjoy the boiled crustaceans and ripe rambutans. Even Mari sang and her song was golden in the darkness. Mahsa joined her in singing and we all listened quietly.

It was only right before dawn that Maria was discovered to be missing.

SHE HAD BEEN CURLED up next to me. I remembered we spoke. Our lips met, caressed bare skin and nuzzled the small of our necks. In the not-so-private world of *Sri Matahari,* we held on to our space bravely, defiantly, passionately. Our hands stroked our soft pubic mounds, eliciting soft sighs. The men had given us room, as usual.

We spoke about going back home, back to the islands of the archipelago. We wanted to explore the Nusantara. We also spoke about marriage, not the formal one, because I knew we just couldn't. We would join hands, exchange vows, witnessed only by ibu and Halim, my closest family. Ibu had never met Maria. But ibu would love her, just like another daughter. We would not be able to produce the grandchildren she so wanted. We spoke, too, about adopting the girl babies often abandoned at the doorsteps of temples and shrines. We would form our own family in the way we wanted.

Maria had entwined her fingers with mine. She smelled deliciously of coconut oil, used to coat her hair and keep it soft. Oddly enough, she smelled more of jasmine. There were no jasmine buds onboard *Sri Matahari.*

I dozed off listening to her breathing. And for a while, my sleep was dreamless.

THEN SHE WAS GONE.

Chapter Nine

MAHSA WAS GONE TOO. The baby dragon was not swimming around *Sri Matahari* either. Even the swarms of fish and fish fry that normally accompanied her had disappeared.

There was no trace, no sign that Maria had left. Her footprints ended at the edge of the riverbank.

I was frantic with panic. I couldn't find her. I couldn't find her at all. All the men shut their mouths and looked at their feet sheepishly. They knew what to do when their kapitan's temper was roused.

"Mari!" I cried. Hot tears were running down my cheeks. "Maria!"

I splashed into the river, thinking to myself she must have taken a bath or swam. *Or drowned,* I cried softly. Mari was a good swimmer. Nothing. No sign of her. How did she just walk into the water and disappear?

Something glistened on the water. Silver-white scales, the size of a Ming coin.

I picked one up. It was tough and fragile-looking like a fish scale, translucent and yet solid. It glowed in my hands. Mahsa. Mahsa. Mahsa.

"Captain, look." Halim's firm voice woke me from my dazed reverie. I felt so lost. Halim's voice was a firm smack on my face. "Scales . . . like a trail."

"Follow the trail." I gritted my teeth. "We go look for Maria. Now."

LIKE A HUNTING DOG, *Sri Matahari* followed the trail, her nose fixed to the scent unwaveringly. I stared at the scales; it would seem Mahsa was shedding one or two, sometimes a cluster. Was there a struggle? A fight? Did someone else capture Mahsa . . . and Maria? Was Mahsa shedding her scales deliberately, to help us find them?

I didn't care about the ever-changing scenery. My wish to go home was gone: all I wanted was to find Maria. I did not eat. I did not drink. I only stared, unblinking, frantically, at the water, looking for hope. Any hope.

"Kapitan, there!" Abdullah yelled.

It wasn't . . . Maria or Mahsa. But a ship, looking eerily like a perahu. *Sri Matahari*'s twin. On the bow stood a figure, hands on the hips. I could feel the aggressive glare from where I was, a burning against my skin. My sharp eyes could see that the figure was slender, clad in similar clothing like ours. Even a headdress, a tanjak, like mine. But the features seemed blurry. I could not see the eyes nor mouth. A fellow traveller from the Golden Chersonese, then. Were they brought here by a similar weather event, or were they veteran adventurers?

The captain … I assumed it was the captain … They stood with a confidence I found unsettling. Like me, when I first became the captain of *Sri Matahari*. Ready to take on everything, cocky, arrogant, the master of their own ship. Invincible.

And inexplicably, the ship turned and sailed away. It felt like a snub.

"This is odd," Halim noted. "They look like lanun from Nusantara. Why don't they render help?"

"We *are* lanun. Some are less generous and more vicious in nature. You know that already, Halim," I said. Even my words felt odd. Empty.

It made no sense. I kept thinking it was all an illusion. A mirror.

"Ah," Halim grunted and turned to give orders to the men to go back to their duties.

I went back to our original task: looking for Maria.

Strangely enough, the trail of silver scales seemed to point towards where the ship had gone. This was going to be interesting.

I FOUND HALIM LIGHTING one of his smokes. It was a sign that he was struggling with something and needed something to distract him. He had been rationing his smokes.

"Kapitan." Halim took a puff and released the aromatic white smoke. It streamed like dragon's breath. "I never told you about Chaiya."

"You never did," I said. *Sri Matahari* rocked gently. I squatted down beside him. "What happened at Chaiya?"

"I was very young then. Just joined your father as crew. We were marooned at Chaiya. The inhabitants were less than welcoming." Halim had a faraway look now. "Some of the Tai tribe. They killed a few of us that day. Never did I see so much destruction."

"They were never trusting of outsiders, foreigners. But now I see that they have changed. Things are different now." Halim's voice trailed off.

"Halim, I am sorry . . ." I said softly. My first mate held up his right hand. It was gnarled and creased. An old but still muscular hand. What else had it seen and felt?

"I have held my tongue for long now. Us chasing the Nak now . . . It reminds me of Chaiya. The danger and the mistrust. I don't like the danger and mistrust. I worry for you, Kapitan. I worry for Maria too. She is dabbling in something of the unseen, of the spirit world. You cannot make bets with spirits. They are treacherous and unreliable. You cannot make deals with celestial beings either. They move in their own way of thinking. "

"I know," I replied, feeling the chill once more.

FROM HERE THE RIVER became more treacherous, riddled with rapids which made sailing so much more dangerous. Thanks to Abdullah's steering and the concerted efforts of the men physically having to guide the ship through the rocks while risking their lives, *Sri Matahari* was able to sail. I was terrified that we had lost the trail, watching the foaming water for any telltale sign of silver.

After careful searching with Halim's experience brought into play, we found the trail once more. Did that particular ship go through the rapids too? And why? There were no signs of their presence. *Sri Matahari* had lost bits of wood trying to navigate the hard rocks. It was as if the other ship had an expert navigator and crew, and had gotten away fairly unscathed. Were they just terribly lucky? Had it sprouted legs somewhat and climbed its way upwards?

Things were not making sense.

They had not made sense ever since Maria found the Naga

THE RIVER SEEMED TO narrow then, into a calmer inlet stream. It should have been broadening by then, if we had kept to our original plan, leading into the delta and then into the sea. Yet, because we were following the trail of silver scales (and a strange lanun perahu), the river had shrunk, though still as fast-flowing as ever. The number of villages seemed to have dwindled and the landscape grew isolated, more wild and unpredictable. At certain times, the tops of the tall soaring trees were covered in white mist. It was also much colder.

Around us rose hills. From my angle, they looked like mountains. Maybe they *were* mountains. Their peaks were hidden in mist and cloud. At times, the clouds rumbled and flickered with lightning.

"What strange sorcery is this?" Halim said, rubbing his hands for warmth. Unused to the sudden chill, he had wrapped a sarong around his neck. "This is bad. Very bad." He glanced at me and I was reminded of our brief conversation about spirits and the unseen. We were indeed in the realm of the unseen world. To reinforce the ominous surroundings, we heard hoots. The sounds echoed and echoed.

The men were commenting that this was the realm of Hanuman. And indeed I believed them.

Large butterflies with tails in their wings fluttered up in waves from the silt-covered earth as *Sri Matahari* sailed past. They were dark-colored and big as birds. In the deeper recesses of the mist-covered trees echoed the sounds of monkeys. The men found any sarong they could find to wrap around their shoulders. As day slid into night, and *Sri Matahari* was forced to anchor, fireflies lit the sky in huge numbers. I wanted to sail in the dark; we shouldn't lose the trail. Maria! Oh, my Mari. But the lives of more lay in my hands. The sky remained clear and the stars shone through like diamonds.

Follow the stars.

Follow the trail of silver.

A shimmering band crossed the sky. I saw the Seven Sisters. I saw the bridge of so many stories told.

Oh, let this be a good sign.

Halim had often scoffed about signs. So did I. We were not fishwives. But ... now I was grasping at signs as if they were good luck charms.

At night, I missed the solid presence of Maria, the hint of her perfume and oils she used. My mat was empty, cold. I couldn't sleep. I missed her bare skin, the sound of her breathing.

The next morning found us back on the trail. The scales were getting scarcer now, as if Mahsa had shed less. Did Nagas even molt? Was Mahsa ... injured?

Mari.

Maria.

The thought of the strange lanun hurting Maria burnt in my soul. I wasn't sure how I linked them to Maria's disappearance, but it felt logical. They must have kidnapped her or something. Caught Mahsa too, for profit. Behaving just like any lanun would ...

For profit.

I wept.

EARLIER ON, WAY EARLIER, when Maria first joined the crew and became a permanent member, we made a promise to sail the Nusantara and the Golden Chersonese together. She had steadfastly refused to go back to her old life, that of indentured service and abuse. I became her family, the crew her uncles and brothers. I had bought her new clothes, even the elegant silk shoes worn by the aristocrats of faraway Europe. Clad in them, she told me she was a new person. She still kept the kebaya and sarong she had worn in that life, a tactile and physical memory she couldn't erase and forget. Her beaded slippers she kept too, locked away, another painful memory.

"I am both Kristang and Peranakan," she had said. "I cannot be one person."

She folded the kebaya and placed it in the cedar box. The box closed with a click. An act of finality.

"As much as I hated her, Bibik molded me into who and what I am today."

She seemed to have reconciled the two within her. She had found peace. More so when she had avenged the deaths of her parents by killing a man. Ever resourceful, she had taught the men how to reuse things. It was part of her past. Bibik did not like to see food waste.

Alongside me, Maria fought as passionately and as ferociously with her saber and dagger. We spared the innocents. We killed the ones who deserved death. I remembered the times she gave food and additional clothing for the coastal villages ravaged by lanun attacks. She understood poverty; she had known and deeply experienced the desperate bite of hunger, of loss.

My saint. My bodhisattva. My light.

I had been alone before. I had sworn to be alone, shutting myself away from emotions. After I had met Maria, I never wanted to be alone again. I saw a future for both of us. We would grow old together. We could have a family together.

Now it seemed that dream was impossible.

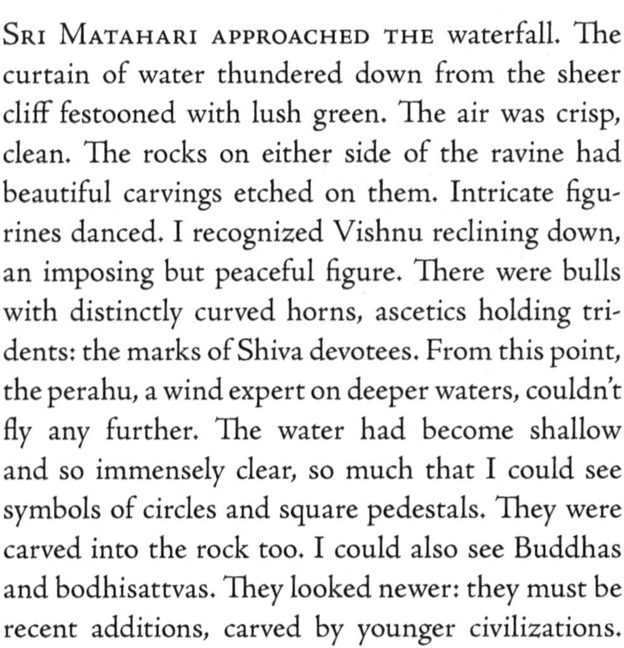

Sri Matahari approached the waterfall. The curtain of water thundered down from the sheer cliff festooned with lush green. The air was crisp, clean. The rocks on either side of the ravine had beautiful carvings etched on them. Intricate figurines danced. I recognized Vishnu reclining down, an imposing but peaceful figure. There were bulls with distinctly curved horns, ascetics holding tridents: the marks of Shiva devotees. From this point, the perahu, a wind expert on deeper waters, couldn't fly any further. The water had become shallow and so immensely clear, so much that I could see symbols of circles and square pedestals. They were carved into the rock too. I could also see Buddhas and bodhisattvas. They looked newer: they must be recent additions, carved by younger civilizations.

The artwork was fascinating; the craftsmanship was meticulous. Orange winged butterflies carpeted the clay. As *Sri Matahari* moved closer, they flew up, like lit embers swirling skywards. In a pool, the silver scales swarmed and swirled. This was where the trail of silver had ended.

I was not surprised to see the other perahu, anchored, right in front of the waterfall. I thought it was a bizarre decision on the part of the captain to anchor next to a column of fast-falling water. Shouldn't it be dangerous? I would have steered *Sri Matahari* away from it. Any self-respecting and astute captain would have.

Why in this place? The air had the air of a sacred temple. Peaceful, calm and holy. Yes, that was the word: holy. The carvings on the rocks were evidence.

"Kapitan!"

Halim's shocked voice.

There, on the bow of the twin ship, stood a very familiar figure.

My heart soared and then plummeted.

Maria.

Chapter Ten

"MARI!" She was clad in her kebaya and sarong, the ones she had kept in the box on board of *Sri Matahari*. How did she manage to get it out? She stood as if she was in a daze, swaying unsteadily on her feet. She was looking—and not—at me. Instead, her eyes were fixed on the other figure next to her. She did not hear me. She was held entranced.

My blood ran cold.

The figure smirked at me.

I was staring at myself.

IT WAS A NIGHTMARE made real.

My evil twin mirrored me in every way, right down to what I wore on my head. That other me had such arrogance about them that I cringed. Their eyes burned with a feverish feral brightness. And instead of short dark hair, it was . . . green.

Sea green.

My hair stood on the nape of my neck. I wanted to scream.

"Let her go," I shouted.

"Why should I?" The evil twin shouted back. The nightmare continued. I must be dreaming. My nails drew blood and pain on my palm. I had clenched my fist tightly. My nails had pierced through skin. The pain brought me back. It was real. It was very real. With some effort, I lifted my hand up and tasted my blood. It too brought me back to the present.

"Who are you?" I yelled, summoning all my strength and courage. Maria appeared more listless now. Was she drugged? My heart grew hot. I felt the fury returning. "What are you?" I didn't know what made me say this. The green hair?

Green.

Green scales, the colour of sea waves.

Sea green.

No, it couldn't be.

"Let Maria go," I repeated. "Your child is safe. I brought her back, as promised. Let Maria go."

Halim flung me a startled glance, before he blinked and nodded to himself. He connected the dots. The men, with their blades in their hands, gasped. Yet, they stood still, unwavering in their courage and defense.

"My child is safe? You took my child!" the green-haired captain said, their eyes burning brighter, like two stars. It was so unnatural, watching myself. I was looking at a twisted version of myself. I wanted to turn away. I couldn't. I shouldn't. For the sake of Maria's life, I stared back.

"Maria saved your child's life. She took care of your egg. She rescued it from the storm."

My evil twin snarled at me.

"She looked after your child! Why do you want to punish her? If you want to punish anyone, punish me!" I countered back.

The green-haired captain stumbled back, as if stung by the truth. The very movement caused a series of reactions.

Maria fell.

This time, I did scream.

Things happened in slow motion.

A surge of water came erupting through the waterfall. I saw the moon appear. No, not the moon. A huge Naga, not as big as the Naga of the dreams, but big nonetheless. Mahsa. She had grown. Even bigger than *Sri Matahari*. Mahsa came, ducking past the mirror perahu, and scooped up Maria with her head.

"Mother," the voice boomed, a rolling thunderstorm. "Stop!"

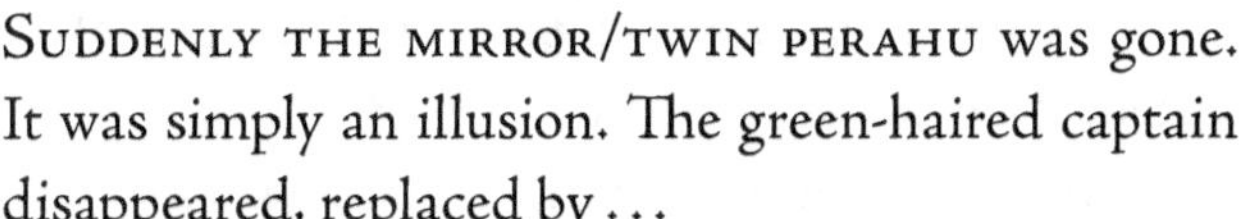

SUDDENLY THE MIRROR/TWIN PERAHU was gone. It was simply an illusion. The green-haired captain disappeared, replaced by ...

The Naga rose, foaming, from the water.

Gleaming like gems, the scales green-blue of the sea, she reared back, her eyes bright, defiant.

"Stop," the younger Naga said, still carefully carrying Maria on her head. If she had arms, she could be cradling Maria tenderly.

We could hear and listen to their speech. It was strange. The sound of storms and winds rustling, with the hint of words. Words that we somehow understood. Words that our hearts understood.

"The manut speaks the truth. They haven't stolen me. She had kept me safe, until I was strong enough to break the shell."

The older Naga rumbled. "You defend them. I do not understand why."

"Indeed I do. They came to this place because of you."

"My child, why do you side with them?"

Mahsa swam right up to her mother. "They wanted to bring me back to you. Why must you abduct her? She rescued me. Why are you punishing her for something she did not do?" There was soft thunder, echoing and vibrating in the ravine.

"She stole you away from me! My child …" For a brief moment, the older Naga looked, for some reason, contrite. Her star-like eyes dimmed. Her head dipped down.

"I like her. She has protected me," Mahsa stated. "She has kept me safe."

With a monsoon roar, the Naga slid back into the water, causing bigger waves and rocking

Sri Matahari. We shouted and held on for dear life. The storm soon abated. The Naga did not return. Instead, Mahsa remained. Gently, slowly, the white Naga swam towards us. And with the same gentleness, she lowered her head and Maria rolled into my arms. She still breathed, her chest rising up and down. She looked as if she was simply sleeping.

"Because she has saved me," Mahsa said, in her rainstorm voice. "She is my temple maiden." The Naga looked down at me, her eyes shining like twin moons.

I shook my head. "No. *No.*"

Mahsa actually looked . . . sad. "She will be safe, with me. I will watch over her and protect her from harm. In my temple, she stands beside me."

This wasn't happening. The nightmare continued. I wanted to wake up.

"Let's hear what Maria says," I said finally.

Chapter Eleven

MARIA WOKE UP IN my arms later.

Her brown eyes met mine, brimming with unshed tears. Her kebaya and sarong were still damp from the ravine's water. Her feet, though, were bare.

"They . . . you . . ." She struggled to speak, struggled to sit up.

"Shhh, you are safe now," I whispered, stroking her brow. She fought me, sitting up, looking around. Whatever had drugged her was gone now: she was clear-eyed.

"They took me," Maria said then, haltingly, before slowly gaining strength. "I knew it wasn't you. But . . . they . . . the Naga! It was the mother Naga pretending to be you!"

"All resolved now," I reassured her, trying to stem my own sadness. It was coming. I was denying it.

"Mahsa!" Maria caught sight of the moon-coloured Naga. The young Nak had been hanging about, watching over Maria worriedly, vigilantly. She then said something in Khmer which was Mahsa's real name. "Preah Chn!" How did she know Mahsa's true name? How did she know the language and speak as fluently as if she was born Khmer? The Nak lowered her head and Maria touched the downward sloping muzzle with a gentle hand. My heart hurt. They did share a special bond.

OUR DISCUSSION ALMOST TURNED into a heated argument. Because of what she had done, her deed that won her merit, Maria was formally blessed as a temple maiden; her eyes shone and she glowed. Oh, my Maria, my precious Mari glowing. With beauty and with pride. Like a star in the sky. Preah Chn promised to look after her as guardian deity. I was angry. Hadn't I protected Mari too?

"I didn't want to leave you too," Maria said, trying to soothe me. "But . . . I made a vow."

"You also made a vow with me," I said. "You did. Why is her vow more important than mine? Ours?"

"Neo . . ." Maria sighed. "I know. But Preah Chn . . . I can't explain this connection I have with her." She pulled me towards her. It was hard to resist, even with how angry I was; my resolve melted before her. She rested her head on my shoulder. My one good shoulder that had not been injured.

"Connection?"

"It . . . it feels like I am flying when I am with her. The joy I feel. The . . ." Maria said breathlessly and stopped when she saw my expression. I knew I frowned, because my forehead felt tight. "No, no . . . I still love you. But . . . it's not the same."

"I just . . . This is all sudden. I don't want you to go." I stroked her hair. "Don't go into the realm of the unseen."

"Six moons, I promise." Maria's voice was soft on my skin. She nuzzled my neck.

"Six moons. That is too long." I stifled my crying. My face was already wet. *I don't want to let you go.*

"You can wait, can't you? I will be back."

"Maria, Mari, don't . . ."

"If you trust me, let me go."

So that was it.

The mother Naga—Samout—accompanied *Sri Matahari* as escort. Her daughter swam beside her. They guided us to the open sea. From there, we could find our way back home. Halim had the map. He had already calculated the route back.

And with this parting, Maria went with the Nagas. She turned back on the head of Preah Chn—now clad in shimmering silver av tronum and sampot, her head wearing an elaborate headdress with intricate silver filigree—and she waved. Around her neck was a garland of white jasmine flowers. At her feet were more flowers. Maria looked like a puteri, a princess. She was now a temple maiden, serving a Naga at her temple. She would stand next to a celestial being. Like the Naga, she would now look after people, not just us.

Six moons.

Six moons was a long time.

Chapter Twelve

WITH MARIA GONE, WE went back to being just . . . lanun. I was listless. Even Halim felt the absence keenly. He missed waking up and preparing the day's meals alongside Maria. Both of them were early wakers. He found himself missing her while he started the fire and the cooking. The routine was broken.

My energy limped. We still engaged in small-time thievery, but it was simply living for the sake of living. Existing for the sake of existing. There was no joy. There was . . .

No Maria.

No Mari.

My joy was gone.

I even delayed visiting ibu. I had so wanted to let Maria see her.

I watched the full moon as avidly as I could. Counting each moonrise. Six moons. She said six moons.

Halim and even Abdullah, the ever-taciturn,

commented tactfully that I had withdrawn into myself. I refused to sit down, as I had always done, with the men after a hard day's work at sea. I preferred my own company, sitting by myself, staring out into the sea, into the sky. I withdrew into myself. The band of silver was still there and somehow I knew Maria was thinking about me. The trail of silver was in my dreams too. This time, not scales, but true stars.

My mat was empty. My heart was hollow. No jasmine and coconut. I became a faint copy of myself, my motions automatic. Halim even suggested we stop sailing for a while, go back to selling wares as merchants. "Let the men go back to their families," he said. "Some of them still do have families."

He said it jokingly, half-contritely, to enliven the mood. He had said before that lanun did not have families. I could only nod numbly.

Maria was my family. Now she was gone.

THE FULL MOONS CAME and went. I noted their risings and settings. And yet, she had not returned. My heart broke. She was gone. She had left me.

THE DAY DAWNED AS any day. I woke up, dreading the sunlight and the prospect of leaving the comfort of my mat. We still needed to go out to sea. *Sri Matahari* still needed to sail. The men needed their pay. Where we had docked, at a small island close to Temasek, the inhabitants had raised lanterns made of paper. They were celebrating Mid-Autumn Festival, they said, a festival from the Middle Kingdom. The kind lady offered me a box of baked round cakes. I smiled and thanked her. The cakes were delicious, filled with green bean paste. They were celebrating the rise of the full moon.

We had hunted as we did; our rewards were boxes of spices and bottles of Madeira wine. The wines we could sell. The spices could fetch high prices in the marketplace. We could live comfortably for the rest of the year.

Maria was not here.

The full moon rose, huge and orange. The villagers lit their lanterns. The lanterns danced in the dark while the children played and laughed. They had made their own little lanterns from sticks and paper. One even made one for me.

I lit the lantern. Alone, I sat down on the beach and wept, accompanied only by the glow of the lone lantern.

Then I saw the ship. It was sailing under the full moon, as bright as it too. I saw its familiar shape: the dragon-head ship, from Ang Kor, only now this one was bigger, encrusted with gold and silver and precious stones. I stood up, my heart pounding hard. In my hurry, I knocked the lantern over. It caught fire and became a tiny sun. I felt its warmth.

Maria stood next to the dragon's head. She

wore her kebaya and sarong, her long hair streaming in the sea wind. Beside the ship swam a Nak, glowing white. Preah Chn.

I ran into the water, just as I did a long time ago.

Only this time, I was welcoming her home.

Golden Beads and Eagle Wings

THE COLORS OF DAWN greeted me the moment I opened my eyes. No, they were the colors of the opalescent full moon. A Naga danced in the sky next to it.

In my arms, Maria stirred slightly and then she went back to a deeper sleep. She smelled of jasmine this time. When she came back, they had woven jasmine buds into her hair. I basked in the fact that I held a moon maiden, a servant of a sacred creature, a Naga. A Nak straight out of the Khmer Lands.

Seeing a Naga now in the Golden Chersonese was uncommon, much less being chosen by a dragon held in high regard by all across the Nusantara and the Khmer Lands. Nak. Naga. It was a beast that guarded the skies and the rivers. It stood sentinel at the gates of temples and shrines. Now there was a white Naga, the color of the moon and the best of pearls, in the sky.

Maria was finally back and I could now sleep.

PREAH CHN WAITED PATIENTLY, her trailing beard gleaming like pearlescent colors, while Maria dressed. This time, Maria put on the clothing she used to wear on *Sri Matahari*: tanjak and batik trousers, the garb of a lanun or pirate. No more garb of the temple maiden, a princess of the moon shrine.

With reluctance and such sorrow, she then placed a gentle hand on Preah Chn's muzzle. The Naga closed her glowing gemlike eyes and the two seemed to commune in their own secret language. I felt a quick pang of jealousy and squashed that emotion. It is not always all about me, I thought.

I was not the one who saved Preah Chn. Mari did.

To Mari, she was always Mahsa.

With a high, fluting voice that even brought tears to the eyes of the hardened lanun watching the odd ceremony, Mahsa sang and slowly reared up. The water around her serpentine form frothed and bubbled, turning into fresh, clean water. Lotus flowers suddenly appeared and bloomed pink and bright, as big as my head. The sea had suddenly turned into a lake filled with pink lotus flowers.

"Preah Chn has released me from my temple duties. She says she will always be there," Maria said in a subdued voice. "But I have made my decision: I will be lanun, with you."

Such sober words. The Maria I had known had seemed to change a lot. After our journey to the Khmer Lands and then the series of events that made her the chosen of the Naga, Maria was more measured. Mature. My Maria, my Mari, had changed. But then, I too had changed.

We had all changed.

Mahsa left us with riches, though. With the wealth, we did not need to hunt and raid again. But I was restless. I wanted to go back to my old life.

Trailing silver light, the sacred Preah Chn flew back to the celestial heavens. She would watch over us as she promised.

WITH THE BEAUTY AND grandeur finally fading away, we went back to the sea. I made the decision to go home, to see ibu and visit her. When we arrived at the door, ibu was surprised to see us, bursting into tears. We gave her the riches from our voyages. She was grateful for the gift and blessed us. She was amazed to see Maria and loved her immediately, accepting her as her daughter. She had the kitchen make us food and drink, and bade us sit down and rest. She greeted Halim like an old friend and gave the men food as well. The hall rang with our voices and laughter. Because she came from a family of shipwrights, she had her repairmen examine *Sri Matahari.*

"The ship needs a lot of repairs," ibu said with a frown. "Whatever they did was good, such meticulous attention. Where did you find them, child?"

"Somewhere," I said.

"I recognized different materials," ibu said. "Now, eat—Halim obviously didn't cook well enough to feed all of you."

"I did my best, ma'am." Halim bowed and they both laughed. Obviously it was some private joke between both of them.

I tucked in with relish. The kari was all I remembered: hot and creamy in my fingers. Maria ate, overwhelmed by the attention.

"She's so unlike Bibik," Maria whispered to me.

"She is not Bibik," I said.

For a long time, I went back to my own room. Ibu had kept it clean, with fresh mats. She had aired the room. Maria joined me, holding my hand, while I looked around, experiencing a flood of unfamiliar emotions. I was home, was I? Had I grown bigger? It felt like a room of my childhood. In a wooden teak cupboard, ibu still kept my old clothes. Mostly men's clothing, a few women's clothing here and there. She had folded them neatly. The wooden carved blades on the wall. The mat for a bed, with the old familiar mosquito netting. The huge globe, now turning yellow with age. Father had purchased it from a merchant. I had spent time admiring and touching it. So many places. So many lands unexplored. The small stack of parchments on the low wooden desk.

"This is your room," Maria said. "You have your own room."

"You didn't?" I looked at her. She was looking around, impressed by the items in the room.

"I had to share with the other servants. And besides, Bibik snored."

"Ah."

That night, we slept in my old room. I suddenly missed the rocking of *Sri Matahari*.

IBU WANTED TO BUILD a new house for us, with brick and mortar. Her wizened face, worn down by time and laughter, beamed with happiness. I promised her we would be back once more, to formally celebrate our union.

A new house.

A new life.

"You take care of her," ibu said, jabbing her thin finger on my chest. "You take care of her, remember? I cannot afford to lose you and her."

"Ibu," I said, touched by her words.

"You are not getting younger either, no spring chicken," ibu chuckled softly. "And you will have a new house! With stone stilts!"

"Ibu!"

"I want to see you both back. What a celebration we will have. You take care of Maria, remember?" Ibu jabbed her finger on my chest again. Then she embraced me gently.

The sea beckoned. My life was built on it. With the sea wind on my face, I was most alive. With so many moons lost, I was ready.

MARIA GAVE ME A Buddhist rosary of golden amber beads. In the sun, they were balls of light on my palm. I was not religious nor was I ever spiritual, but I kept the rosary close to me, next to my chest. They were a physical reminder of Mari.

We left Ibu's home and the island, albeit reluctantly. Ibu warned Halim not to be derelict in his duties as first mate. Halim only nodded quietly.

We went back to the raids. The takings were good as usual: with the extra luck, we were earning more than normal.

Yet, for some reason, I was not happy. I felt as if I was still walking wounded, something having been removed physically from me. The raids would give me joy, but the joy was often brief. I was left feeling as if an emptiness had descended upon me. A dark and sobering emptiness. Visiting and seeing ibu only reinforced the emptiness. Was I longing for home? Longing to settle down for good?

Maria could only hold me in her arms and say nothing. Her brilliance shone and I felt dull beside her. She had surpassed me. I could not blame her. We both had changed.

I ended up holding the beads in my hand,

letting my fingers rub each bead. The repetition calmed me. My shoulder throbbed, a memory of an old injury. Why it had even bothered to act up now was a mystery. I had Maria. I had *Sri Matahari*. I was a successful lanun. I was still young, or so I thought. What was wrong with me?

LIFE MOVED ON. THE ship had to be repaired. The men had to be paid. We sold some of the goods. It was just motion now. Automatic, like breathing or eating. I was almost convinced I was back to normal, whatever normal was. I strove to enjoy this temporary contentment.

It was a hot afternoon, when the sun had begun its downward descent, when we heard the fight in the sky. We were coasting along, *Sri Matahari* having caught a sea wind. There was no raid planned and everyone was at leisure. The men repaired sails and nets, while Halim and Abdullah discussed docking at the nearest island to us. Mari served as lookout, something she insisted she wanted to do. We had a roster in place, but Mari could be extremely stubborn. So we let her and she watched the waters keenly.

The fight was loud enough to draw all eyes to the sky. Loud squawking and honking. Two eagles dueled. Even from the distance, I knew they were sea eagles. Lang siput, as the islanders would call them. They were revered by indigenous people who lived along the coasts. One looked to have darker feathers. The one with the lighter plumage was an adult and primed with fiercer talons and even fiercer temperament. It darted about the younger eagle, lashing out with beak and talon. The younger bird wobbled in its desperate flight. Feathers had begun falling. The older bird had been tearing at it.

The adult lunged and his opponent squawked out. We heard its pain.

It tumbled from the sky.

The older bird flapped away, catching the hot air before soaring further into the heavens. I watched the younger bird fall . . .

. . . and it hit the wooden deck with a thud, of the sickening sound of brittle broken bones, and a mass of bloodied brown grey feathers.

Maria yelled something.

The eagle had fire in its dark eyes. Its curved talons, already as sharp as an adult's, twitched spasmodically. I stayed well away from them. It was still alive. Only that blood matted its right wing and continued to drip on the deck in a steady red stream.

"Shh," I reassured the bird. I felt a little ridiculous talking to a bird. "Bring me clean cloth and water."

"Kapitan," Halim said. "We are not eagle hunters."

"Bring me clean cloth," I repeated. "And water."

I CARRIED THE JUVENILE sea eagle to the sheltered hold. It was surprisingly light. Blood got all over my hands and arms as it kicked at me with its talons. I carefully wrapped the clean cloth around the wounded shoulder and wing, taking care to cover its eyes with more cloth. I cleaned the wounds with the water. Even then, the eaglet tried to peck me. But it was weak from the duel and the wounds. I kept thinking it was a he. I tried to avoid his talons. I removed the cloth from the head. Its eyes glared at me with murder. When Halim approached the eagle, it snapped at him.

Maria watched, amazed and with curiosity.

"We need to make sure it does not move too much. And it needs fresh food," I said.

Halim looked at the bird doubtfully.

"It's a sign," I found myself saying. "I am going to make sure the bird recovers."

"We are lanun," Halim pointed out. "We don't pay attention to signs." That was a pointed jibe. We had sworn, a month ago, not to pay too much attention to signs.

"Yes," I replied. "We are lanun."

"Signs have nothing to do with lanun," Halim stated flatly. "Remember what I told you."

"Yes, I do. Meanwhile, we have an injured bird," I said and left it at that.

Later, Halim managed to catch flying fish with the net we had repaired. He cut up the fish into chunks, including the orange egg sac, and I placed them in front of the eaglet. They remained untouched.

I changed the bandage and made a poultice from our supplies of herbs and plants picked from our most recent island forage. I pounded the herbs into a mash with a stone. With the eaglet squawking loudly, I applied the green paste on the wound, before bandaging it up again. The wound had to hurt. I hoped the paste helped reduce the swelling.

"We are not eagle hunters," Halim shook his head. "Maybe we should change our profession, eh? The tribesmen told me that the eagles helped them hunt fish."

I ignored the gentle sarcasm. "Get me soft pulp or cork wood, anything you could find," I said firmly. I smelled of blood and bitter herbs. I needed to bathe.

"Kapitan?"

"We need to cover up those talons."

HALIM THOUGHT THE SEA eagle would become a liability and give our position away with its squawking. It was a miracle or a few that we were able to hunt and raid, without even disturbing the eaglet. He lay, head tucked against his good wing. His eyes watched us. The men left him alone. Halim treated the bird like some novelty. Maria tried to help with the food, sneaking in bits of fish. The eagle pecked at them desultorily.

I gradually felt better. The dark emptiness seemed to have lifted. It was still there, flexing its claws. But I did not feel as bad as before.

From the merchant ships we had captured boxes of wine, celadon, Ming porcelain, pepper and more silks. These silks were more wool-like: they were made from silk worms from the wild. The cocoons were harvested after the moths had emerged, not boiled. Maria said they were called ahimsa silk. Peace silk. So unlike the silk made from the Khmer Lands where they bred the worms. The silks would make good shawls.

We sold the wine and I bought clean cotton linen with the coins.

"We leave the bird with someone who can look after it," Halim advised.

"For now, we look after the bird," I said. I had privately named the eaglet Biru. Already his adult plumage was emerging: more blue and light grey.

After a few days, Biru had begun to eat, much to my and Maria's relief. He gobbled up the fish chunks and looked for more. He seemed to have more energy now, getting back to his talons. He pecked futilely at the pulp covering the tips of his talons, more surprised than angered. I planned to find bamboo tubes for those claw tips. But cork wood should suffice for now. At least Biru had not clawed anyone. Yet.

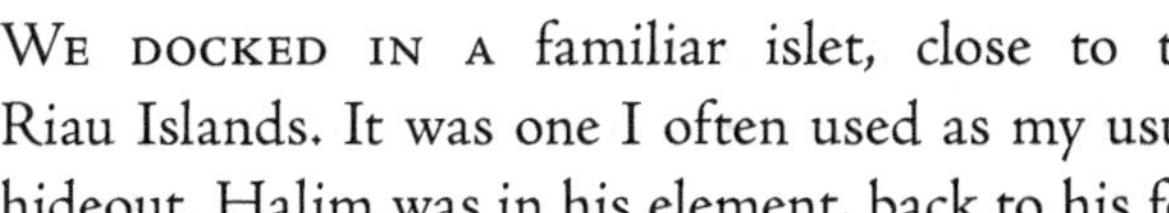

WE DOCKED IN A familiar islet, close to the Riau Islands. It was one I often used as my usual hideout. Halim was in his element, back to his foraging and harvesting. To my pleasant surprise, he found a plant that promoted wound healing. "For the bird," he said awkwardly before heading back to the shallows to look for fresh clams and latok. He could later make a cold salad out of the clams and the sea grapes with whatever vinegar we had left in the hold.

Biru was more alert now, his eyes darting about and watching everything with keen interest. I fashioned him a perch from an ironwood branch I'd picked up. One of the driftwood Mari so loved. Biru perched right on it, bopping his head.

"See how he watches you," Maria whispered reverentially. "Such a beautiful bird."

I was tempted to reach out to touch Biru's neck. He was a wild animal. I was careful not to become too comfortable. Biru was no tame animal.

While we ate our evening meal, Biru's eyes followed our movements. I gave him some fish scraps. His curved beak darted out, snatched the scraps and he tossed his head, swallowing the fish.

IN THE COMING WEEKS, Biru's wing healed and he grew out his brown juvenile feathers. Down feathers covered *Sri Matahari*'s deck. "We look as if we are defeathering chicken," Halim said.

I removed the linen bandage. The wound had closed neatly, without hint of infection. Biru spread his huge wings, testing them gingerly at first, and then with more confidence. We felt the rush of wind as he worked them. Such power and such beauty. Biru would leave eventually, I knew.

For some strange reason, word started going about the "captain with the sea eagle." People had seen me and the sea eagle in our perahu. I shrugged it off. Biru was not my pet.

It's a sign.

But we were lanun: we did not believe in signs.

It was after a fairly uneventful hunt (the pickings were lean at this time of the season) when Biru suddenly decided to perch on my left arm.

Without warning, he flapped his wings and hopped onto my bare arm. I let out a yelp. I felt the claws dig in, immediately thankful that the tips were covered by cork wood. Still I felt the power, the sheer weight of the sea eagle. I was not built stocky nor was I tall. Yet I held Biru without faltering. His dark eyes locked straight into mine. I winced softly as his weight did something to my injured shoulder. Pain ran up my arm.

"Neo!" Maria gasped.

"Shhh!" I said, cautioning her.

He might have thought I was just another perch. But those eyes *knew*. Were aware. He could identify us by sight.

Halim rushed up to see what the commotion was, halted in his paces and simply stared.

"Sea eagle captain," Halim laughed, breaking the silence. "You fit the growing myth."

Signs and now myths. I glared at him. Biru

cocked his head briefly, before hopping off back to his driftwood perch.

BIRU GREW BOLDER, PERCHING on my arm more frequently. At the same time, I started talking to Maria, about our future. A house was being built. Maria had always wanted to adopt children, especially girl children, abandoned by their parents because they were born girls. We had spoken about this. Now it felt more pertinent.

"Ibu is building a house," I said, "for us."

"Our lives. Together." Maria smiled. Once more, she was my Maria. My Mari.

"Yes, I think . . . it's time to think about our lives after a life at sea."

"How about your restlessness? You never wanted to settle down."

"I am still young, but . . ."

"See, you just don't want to settle down."

I sighed. The conversation verged dangerously close to an argument. I had to steer it away from the potential danger. Mari was right: I didn't want to settle down, because I still cherished the sense of freedom being at sea.

"Are you still angry with me? For leaving you?" Maria's next few words startled me. They were laced with a profound sadness.

"No," I said quickly. "No, no, no."

"Halim told me you were . . . not eating, not even doing what you are good at . . ."

"Being a pirate?"

"Why . . . yes. You were not yourself."

"I wasn't."

"You were angry then?" she circled back to her original subject. Why did she still feel that I was angry with her? Why must she always be so afraid of my anger?

I cursed the Bibik who did irreparable damage to this precious and beautiful soul.

"I . . ." I held her trembling hand. "I was. I was angry and sad that you left. Then it was just sadness for a while. I am not angry with you now."

"I am sorry," Maria said, lowering her head. I could see tears rolling down her cheeks.

"You saved Mahsa. You became her chosen servant. You did what you could. I am proud of you."

"But I made you sad."

"That's the past now. We look to the future. Our future. Mari, you are a different person now, you have grown so much. You shouldn't let the past get to you."

Maria sighed, looking out into the setting sun. The sky lit up with orange and red. One of the men had brought out his mouth harp and was playing a tune.

"You are not yourself, of late," Maria said finally. "It's not the sadness I feel inside you. It's something else. Something deeper. What's wrong, Neo?"

The emptiness. She had sensed the emptiness,

of course. Had never spoken about it and now she was confronting it. Confronting me, gently, lovingly.

"I feel as if there is an emptiness in me, a loss of direction," I confessed. "I feel rudderless."

"Perhaps Biru is your new purpose. Perhaps there is more than just being lanun."

"Mari, I really do not know. It feels like uncharted seas before me."

She leaned on my chest. "You have a direction and you have a chart, within you. You just have to find it."

"You sound confident," I said into her hair.

"Ibu is glad that she has another daughter," I said, changing the topic. I had become ibu's son. She had accepted the change in me.

"She fed me so much food!" Maria giggled then. "Let's talk about our future. Maybe that's the direction you are missing." I smiled. Perhaps, like Maria, I should not let the past get to me too. I was not the same gangly teenager who set out to sea with their father's trusted retainer. Not anymore.

We talked about the house and what we wanted to put in there. I was hesitant. I was too used to *Sri Matahari* and travelling light. Yet Mari's presence was a gentle warmth and I found myself nodding off to sleep.

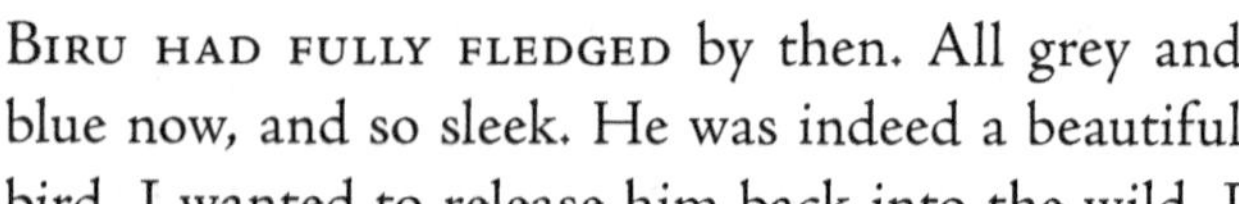

BIRU HAD FULLY FLEDGED by then. All grey and blue now, and so sleek. He was indeed a beautiful bird. I wanted to release him back into the wild. I had to. He belonged to the sea. He was all healed now and his wingspread was enormous. When he beat them, I felt the air shift.

"Go, you," I said gruffly. Biru sat stubbornly on my arm. "Just go."

Biru kekked at me, rustling his ruff and bobbing his head. I had removed the pulp from the talon tips. Instead I wrapped cloth around my forearm. His claws sank in. I felt them. Yet they had not drawn blood.

"You are fully healed! Go, you!"

Biru bobbed his head again.

"You are wild. You belong to the sky and the sea. You can't stay here!"

With flapping wings, Biru lifted from my arm. His feathers brushed my face. I could feel the sheer power of the wings. I was relieved he could fly. He now picked up enough wind to soar higher into the air. He circled for a while, before flying off. My eyes were hot with unshed tears. For a moment, I genuinely thought he had indeed bonded with me. Was mine. Was never mine.

"There she goes," Maria said. "Goodbye, Biru." She waved sadly.

"She?" I said.

"I think . . . I think Biru is actually female. Halim was telling me about how to differentiate between the sexes. She's big, unlike a male eagle."

"Huh," I said. "Now *she's* back to the wild."

With a sharp pang in my heart, I realized I was going to miss Biru.

Shaking my head, I turned to Abdullah. "Onwards, we sail. Today we should reach Karimunbesar."

We had wanted to reach Karimunbesar for more supplies and to trade with the merchants there.

"Aye," Abdullah said briskly. "Uh, Kapitan, your eagle is coming back."

"*My eagle?*" I said tartly, but I instinctively looked skywards.

My eagle. The men all thought Biru was my eagle.

Indeed, Biru was circling above the perahu, calling out softly. Before I knew it, she had dipped down and flew towards me. Then she landed on my left arm, with a soft satisfied squawk, and began preening. She looked very pleased with herself. Her talons dug into my skin, but they did not pierce it. I was surprised at the level of restraint shown by Biru. But Biru was Biru.

"I guess she wants to stay," Maria said, her eyes twinkling.

Halim began to laugh and the men joined him.

⌒⌒

"You are not my eagle," I told Biru when I carried her off to her perch.

The sea eagle looked at me with her dark eyes.

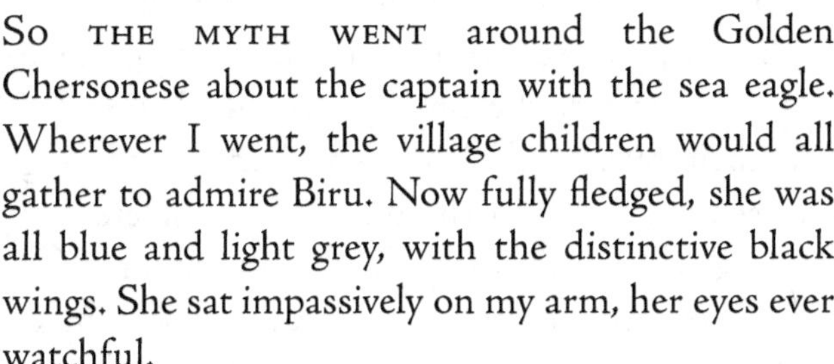

So the myth went around the Golden Chersonese about the captain with the sea eagle. Wherever I went, the village children would all gather to admire Biru. Now fully fledged, she was all blue and light grey, with the distinctive black wings. She sat impassively on my arm, her eyes ever watchful.

"Can we touch it?" the children would ask with shining eyes. Biru stoically endured the attention.

By now, many moons had passed by. We were finally back in business. I felt strong, vigorous. The name of *Sri Matahari* was being mentioned everywhere. We had crates and crates of goods, precious stones and even weapons of orang asing make. Dutch and English pistols fetched hefty prices. Halim persuaded a blade seller to take in a consignment of French sabers. The exchange was fruitful. Mari donated the precious stones to the temples and shrines, so that they could feed the orphans and children who came to them to be looked after. For a while, things were good. We explored the archipelago more, ducking in and out of the many islands. We were chased by a couple of orang asing ships, but we paid them back with raids. We visited our Orang Laut friends with gifts. They welcomed us back with feasts and a generous flow of arak.

Biru seemed to protect me. When we fought with other lanun or merchant sailors, she could rake the men with her curved talons. She was fast becoming quite infamous. *The terror bird.* In turn, I too became infamous. Gossip flowed just as quickly as the tides. Eager ears and mouths exchanged stories, and most of the time, people liked to embellish their tales. Biru had somewhat grown fangs and sharper claws in the tall tales, complete with flaming eyes and a wingspan that hid the sun.

I was growing content, however. Had I finally found my direction? Did my emptiness go away?

During our brief sojourns back on the shore, Maria went about looking for fabrics. She wanted to make a special kebaya. It was such a joyous time as she explored the textiles markets, caressing the cloth with wondering fingers. I wondered what she was planning and about the secrets behind her shy smile.

Sri Matahari circled back to Madan where the lanun village was. Old friends who had retired or were injured now lived there with their families. At first glance, the village looked like any other sea village of Orang Laut or fishermen. When my perahu slowly sailed in, barefoot children ran up the sandy white beach to greet us. They were lanun's children—born to the sea and knew ships by sight. *Sri Matahari* was a familiar sight and I could hear cheerful "pakcik, pakcik!" coming from the unruly group. "Lang siput, lang siput!" the younger children squealed. They patted Biru and enticed her with fish. The kapitan with the sea eagle was back.

My friends met me in the headman's hut. The headman was, of course, an old lanun, one whom I saw as a mentor, of sorts. He was also a friend of my father's. My father had known many people and made many friends. We shared a feast of spicy fish, white clams and hot rice, plied with moonshine and gossip. They had boiled the fish and clams, heaping them in the middle of the large green palm leaf serving as a plate. Rice was served individually.

I relished the sensation of squishing the rice and fish meat together with my hand, mixing the fiery red sambal in with my fingers. The moonshine was similar to the arak we had onboard *Sri Matahari:* deceptively light like clear spring water and smooth, but fire going down the throat. Drinking it made us tipsy.

Biru watched us as we laughed about old times. She fed on a fresh pomfret, straight out of the sea, tearing into the flesh with her hooked beak while her talons held the fish firmly. The children watched her intently. They had never seen a sea eagle so close before. A couple of them brought more fresh fish, tiny ikan kuning, as some sort of tribute or peace offering.

Later, the feast eased into smokes and more arak. I heard the children playing under the evening sky, their light voices carefree and happy. Close by, Maria ate with the women. They were chatting and laughing, exchanging fronds covered with food.

They were no doubt talking about their husbands and partners.

The sound of the waves and the feeling of home (and the moonshine) lulled me almost into a state of contentment. Perhaps this was what normalcy felt like.

Maria drowsed beside me later that night. Biru perched on an empty wooden crate from the East India Company, a relic of a lanun's past. The eagle tucked her head under her wing and slept. I wondered what she dreamed of.

FOR ME, I DREAMED. The dreams flowed from one scene to another, seemingly all my memories replaying once more. The waterspout. The Khmer Lands. The sounds of the instruments playing as the Naga ship sailed down the river Mekong. The festival of the dead. The sky lanterns floating skywards. The strange twin twisted perahu and its captain. The mother Naga confronting us. The trail of silver scales. The trail of stars. The thundering waterfall.

Suddenly yellow butterflies fluttering up from the silt.

And Mahsa, Preah Chn, glowing bright like the full moon. Mari dressed as a puteri, so regal and remote. She stood on the Naga's head as they headed towards the stars, always the stars. The Bintang Utara shone bright in the sky.

The dreams joined like a necklace. I watched the scenes as they replayed themselves.

And then Mahsa once, this time brighter and closer, slapping the water with her large tail repeatedly, as if she was beating a drum . . .

Was she trying to wake me up? Was there danger?

Her tail beat the water insistently.

THE FRANTIC CLANKING OF metal woke me from a deep sleep. Biru was shrieking, flapping her powerful wings. Maria reached out and grabbed her dagger. She was awake and alert. Together we ran out of the hut, holding our weapons. Men were shouting, a riot of torches and running bodies. They had grabbed whatever weapons they could find. This being a lanun village, most still had their blades from their previous trade.

"Raiders!" Halim came running, holding his kris in his right hand, an axe in his left. I saw small perahus sliding in like dark sharklike shadows. Figures ran up the beach; I glimpsed weapons, snarling mouths.

Biru squawked and flew into the dark sky. Bird instinct. For a brief moment, I thought she had fled. Disappeared for good. The thought smarted. Yet, I could feel the flapping of large wings above. Wise bird. Staying out of danger.

Maria herded the women and children to a safer area, to the scraggly hill that served as lookout for the sentries. The lanun island had maintained the lookout for a long time. They were prone to getting attacked by neighboring islanders. Maria held onto her dagger, her eyes burning with a fierce light I had grown to love and respect.

"Come back to me safe," she whispered before she scrambled up the hill. The women still bore weapons, though, as well as the children. They were of lanun stock and would fight to the death if necessary. They all looked back, unafraid. Some of the women wanted to join the fight. They were pregnant, but unhampered by their condition. "I will protect them."

"We will take care of ourselves," one of the makciks laughed, gesturing with her parang.

I returned to chaos. The raiders were probably lanun, like us, or neighboring villages not afraid to resort to raiding when their food and supplies were low. Or they had already coveted certain things in their targeted village and planned to take, regardless of innocent lives. This time of the year, the rains were delayed and vegetable lands were parched dry. The lanun island still had growing vegetables and greens, something they obviously wanted for their own. It had its own freshwater streams which the women had used to irrigate their fields.

Men were wrestling with one another, blades against exposed throats, blows exchanged, swear words aplenty.

In the turmoil, I could not see Halim,

Abdullah and the rest of the men. Yet I could hear them, Halim's shouts and curses, as they fought like frenzied animals. It sounded like a fight on the sea, except this time, it was on land. We were not on *Sri Matahari* anymore.

Yet the fighting felt the same. A fight to save our lives and defend ourselves.

A shadowy figure came at me and I was able to block his blow with my right arm. I could smell alcohol on his breath—a sharp stale scent that almost made me gag. Did they all drink before they began the raid? Why? The blow's impact vibrated through bone and up my shoulder. My old injury flared up, the pain as sharp as before. I gasped, hot tears running down my face. With a vicious curse, I kicked the figure. He cursed back at me. I was familiar with the dialect. He was insulting my mother. I caught accents: Bugis? Makassar? They too were fearsome warriors and sailors. Why were they doing this?

A shrill shriek came above and claws raked the man's face, causing him to duck down and curl into a fetal position. Biru!

He screamed, yelling about demons and hantu. He covered his face with his hands. Seizing the opportunity, I sank my dao into the man's throat. He gurgled and then died. I pulled out the blade and went into the fray, joined by Biru who raked at men's faces with her talons.

What Halim told me . . . much later, when

the raiders had been chased off and the lanun village counted their living and dead, a narrative was growing about the divine bird accompanying a certain warrior. The divine bird was his protector, a warrior with dark wings and sharpened talons. Like Garuda given form. They chased off the potential attackers, causing deep cuts on the skin. Garuda meting out punishment to the wicked. I had to laugh. I was no Hang Jebat nor was I Hang Tuan.

In the end, I had sustained some cuts on my arms and legs. They were minor cuts, though, while bleeding freely. I was glad we survived the raid. The women and children came down from the hill, reuniting with their husbands and fathers. Maria rushed up and hugged me impulsively, causing Halim to turn red as the sambal we'd eaten during the feast. Biru landed near me—clever bird—and waited patiently until I was attended to by the villager's elderly healer. The women helped with the bandaging and administration of herbal poultices. Then, after a while, they began to clean up the mess. One or two huts had been ransacked. In their flight, they had left one or two small perahus on the beach. The men decided to repurpose them for their own use.

"We might have to put up a barrier of spiked logs at the beach, though I feel as if they would climb the hills if they could," the headman said. He cleaned his blade, clearly relishing the touch of it. "The Makassar are nothing but determined. Why they drank is a mystery only Tuhan could explain.

We could have gladly exchanged food with them. But yet, they came at us with violence."

"As do all sea people," I said. I clasped his arm in a lanun's salute and greeting. "Take care, pakcik. Until we meet again."

"May the sea look after you," the headman said.

Maria was folding clothes when I finally came back to our lodgings. I caught a glimpse of fine light red-brown fabric before she quickly hid it under other folded clothes. Was that her special kebaya? I had found out that she had enlisted the help of a master kebaya maker, an older lady who lived in the same village.

"We will probably leave by first light tomorrow," I said.

"You have barely healed," Maria noted. "See, I can still see blood."

"They are only minor wounds," I said. She had the pursed-lips look again.

"How am I going to explain this to your ibu? You fell down the stairs? You knocked your head against a wall? Bruises and scrapes?"

Her tone was teasing but with a hint of seriousness too.

"She is fully aware of my trade."

My shoulder chose the time to twinge painfully. I winced. Maria saw it, seized the opening, and pressed her argument, brave warrior she was.

"More so she should be worried for you. Did she say you have to protect me? How can you protect me when you are hurt all the time?"

"Good move."

"You are only made of flesh and blood. Mortal. Not invincible. And I hurt when I see you hurt. What did ibu say? You are not a spring chicken anymore. Don't deny it. I was there when she said it."

"I am a lanun."

"So am I. But … we are not invincible, not all the time. Even lanun grow old. Just look at Halim. How many times have you been injured?"

"I lost count," I answered too blithely and regretted my tone. I was behaving like a child, demanding and argumentative. Maria was right: lanun did get old. Halim had more white hair now. Even the pakciks and the lanun living their twilight days on the islands we'd visited. They seemed content with their lot, fishing and talking to their old friends. Was this what I would end up doing?

"Look, I am sorry. I still feel fine. They are minor wounds and they will heal quickly," I reassured her.

Maria came up to me. I smelled jasmine and sandalwood. She lifted my right hand and kissed it gently. I heard a soft kekk from Biru from her perch, as if the sea eagle was also making a point. Oh shut up, Biru.

"I would be happy to be the life-companion and isteri to the sea eagle captain," she finally said.

She spoke the words I wanted to say for a long time. Only that Maria was only Maria: bold and brave, speaking her thoughts aloud. Blunt. Unafraid.

"Isteri to the sea eagle captain." I smiled. "I like that."

Maria smiled back in return. "And?"

"Will you marry me? I have told you that life at sea would be difficult."

She placed a warm hand on my arm.

"The Chinese use red ribbons to symbolize the bond between lovers. I do not have red ribbon now, but I have these"—she took out a necklace of golden amber beads from a cloth pouch—"at the moment."

She slowly, carefully wrapped it around our hands. The golden beads wove around our fingers, joining us together.

"Now we are married," she whispered reverently. "In the eyes of God and the Blessed Virgin, we are joined. Que Deus cuide de nós. The Blessed Virgin and Her angels watch over us."

"Mari." I kissed her back, on the lips. "Oh, Maria Fernandes. My sweet saint." Our union, with a sea eagle as our very first witness. I had my golden beads with me still. My gift from her. I smiled. She had hers all the time. "You have been planning this all this time, haven't you? We have *two* necklaces of golden rosary beads?"

Her eyes twinkled and her smile was suddenly mischievous. "Tsk tsk tsk, I am no saint . . . But yes,

I did all this. We will have the full ceremony when we go to ibu's house, promise? We should celebrate with ibu, Halim and the others."

"I promise."

"Hope she loves sea eagles."

"Hope she loves dragons too."

Mari giggled. "Sea eagles and Nagas."

We kissed once more. This time, we kissed more deeply and longer. We pulled apart, breathless and laughing.

Biru kekked, bobbing her head, and settled down to preen her wings.

WE LEFT FOR HOME the next day, the hold stocked up with supplies and our loot from the raids. I wore my plain tanjak and trousers, my dao tucked in my belt, while Maria stood beside me, similarly dressed. On my left arm Biru perched, unruffled by the sea wind blowing at our faces. She was a sea bird, after all.

A flash of white moon color at the corner of my eye, a flicker of serpentine tail and fin—Mahsa. She kept pace with us.

I smiled. Now we had a Naga escort.

Things were suddenly looking bright.

Epilogue

WE ARRIVED HOME WITH ibu launching into a long tirade of colorful language the moment she saw my blood-stained bandages. She tsk-tsked angrily at Halim whose grizzled faced turned red like a boy who was caught sneaking out of the house. Her temper soon blew over like a sea tempest. She was at least relieved to see Mari unharmed. Ibu fussed over her with food and hot tea, while half-berating me for not looking after her properly.

Ibu kept to her promise and she showed us our house proudly. It was still largely unfurnished, but it was big, in my eyes. Next to the sea, with a grove of coconut palms. It would not suffer from flooding, since it was built on stone stilts. Ibu had them carved from granite. The island she lived on had a quarry. "Even the roof," declared ibu, "will not fly away during storms and monsoons. I used teak and sea almond wood!"

The house indeed was impressive. It was not

Sri Matahari. Would my legs get used to land? Living in a house, built with baked brick and mortar, would take some time of getting used to. As we walked about, admiring the house with its stone stilts, children followed us. They were mostly fascinated by the sight of Biru. They had never seen a sea eagle so tame on someone's arm.

Ibu was surprised to see Biru preening her wings on my good arm. "Oh, I see we have a new friend," she said and fed the sea eagle with strips of fresh white fish. She was more surprised to catch a glimpse of Mahsa. The Naga was swimming around *Sri Matahari*. Lotus flowers were popping up in her swirling wake. "Oh, that's a good sign! You are truly blessed," she exclaimed. Thankfully, ibu did not probe any further, not even about the sea of lotus flowers blossoming spontaneously on saltwater. Ibu was a tactful woman who just accepted things as they were. The towkay's wife was the one everyone always turned to if they wanted to chat.

I privately decided to sit her down one day and tell her about the whole story over hot Ceylon tea, her favorite. I wondered how she would react to the part where we were marooned at Ang Kor by a waterspout and an angry Naga.

It took some time for us to get used to being back on land once more. My wounds quickly healed, to ibu's relief. Then, the preparations began in earnest and the village went all out. For seven days, people ran in and out of ibu's house, getting things ready. Ibu supervised and gave instructions. Maria made the finishing touches to her kebaya. She took out the beaded slippers.

With Halim and ibu as our official witnesses, Maria and I joined our hands in a formal marriage. My heart glowed to see Mari wearing her special kebaya, with intricate embroidery of phoenixes and peony flowers. She was beautiful in red, the phoenixes in golden thread. I wore matching tanjak (also with golden thread) and pants made of ahimsa silk. The night before, ibu drew henna patterns on Maria's hands and feet. All close woman friends and companions had their hands tattooed. They talked all the time while they prepared for the ceremony. Ever creative, they had gathered the lotus flowers from the sea and turned them into bouquets and decorations. The house smelled sweet, perfumed by lotus. Ibu had us bathe in water steeped in flowers as well, so that we could wash away all bad luck. We emerged from the scented bath feeling refreshed anew and smelling fragrant.

Mari wore her silver necklace with the crucifix. She shimmered in the sunlight as she walked down, shyly, the path towards me before the ceremony. The henna turned a deep brown-red on her skin, curling like morning glory vines. She looked like a queen, regal and elegant. Walking into the ceremonial hall to the beat of drums and joined by her maids of honor, she smiled at me.

And for that morning and night, we were treated like royalty, raja and rani, seated on a raised dais with the pink lotus flowers at our feet.

Halim led the prayers and ibu fed us with a feast where she then invited the entire village. There was silat (performed solemnly by Halim) and there was a lot of merry dancing and singing. Ibu even invited the Bajau who had their boats anchored nearby. They brought a large sail fish, still alive and all gleaming silver, as a wedding gift. Ibu had also made friends with the Bugis merchants. Their bissu came and blessed us with sacred songs and benzoin smoke. "Together, you sail," they said. "Together, you will be strong."

Mahsa watched from the sea, dancing in patterns of figure-eights and singing with her high fluting voice. All kinds of sea birds from terns to eagles perched on rocks, trees and roofs. They filled the air with their cries. The sea roiled with fish of various species. Halim told me later that there were even dolphins who spun as they leapt out of the water. There was such a joyous atmosphere that the skies broke out in rainbows. Children stood staring with their mouths open in wonder.

Then, with playful giggles from the bride's entourage and gentle shoving on our backs, we were led to our house. Ibu had prepared our bedroom with fragrant mats woven from pandan leaves and small pillows filled with brown rice husks. Above our head hung an ornate lantern, no doubt yet another gift from her neighbors, traders from the Middle Kingdom who had settled on the island. The lantern cast a gentle orange glow. I loved the painted patterns on it. Ibu said the patterns depicted a moon viewing during the fifteenth day of the month, beloved by the Middle Kingdom. The craftsman was truly a master of his trade. I could see ladies in court gowns lifting their cups to a yellow full moon in the sky. Ibu had also moved the items from my old room to the house. The aging globe with its wooden lion-paw stand stood next to the teak cupboard now filled with both my and Maria's clothing. Where we usually greeted visitors stood the low table, now varnished with a new coat. On the bedroom wall hung the wooden blades. As always, we had new mosquito nets made from the finest cotton. A servant had lit a mosquito coil too. The incense filled the air.

We both wore our golden beads on our wrists like bracelets, symbolizing our union. In the light of the paper lantern, they were tiny suns. We looked at one another and our eyes, too, shone. I kissed Mari's hand lightly. Pushing back the mosquito nets like soft curtains, we stepped onto the mat. We were in our own world, cocooned by the white diaphanous cloth. We slowly undressed, savoring each other by sight and touch, and made sweet love into the sultry night. Outside bats fed on mangos hanging from the trees. The fragrance of ripe mangos joined the pandan and jasmine as our bodies touched and merged. When we finally lay back on the cool mat, our skin glistening with sweat, I gathered a sleepy Mari into my arms, waiting for the sunrise. We would watch it together.

Now I would just enjoy the sound of sea waves

caressing the beach and Mahsa crooning us a sleepy lullaby. Tiny moths flitted about the light of the lantern.

ONE LAST THING:

We made good on the promise that we would adopt girl orphans. The very next day, after we watched the sunrise together as a married couple, we went to the nearby Buddhist temple to adopt two girl children, twin sisters still in their early infancy, just a few months old. They both had tousled curly dark hair, tinged with the faintest of gold. In our arms, they were beautiful. We named them Nura and Qistina: Radiance and Justice. Ibu, now a proud grandmother, gushed over them and dressed them in the finest baju. We asked Halim to be their godfather and he agreed with tears in his eyes. Mahsa would be their celestial guardian and protector. On the day of the adoption, the pool in the Buddhist temple suddenly filled with lotus flowers.

Now we began our new life as a family.

FIN

About the Author

J OYCE CHNG LIVES IN Singapore. Their speculative fiction has appeared in *The Apex Book of World SF II*, *We See A Different Frontier*, *Cranky Ladies of History*, *Multispecies Cities* and *Accessing The Future*. Joyce also co-edited *The Sea is Ours: Tales of Steampunk Southeast Asia* with Jaymee Goh. They wrangle fiction and nonfiction editing at the Hugo-winning *Strange Horizons*. Alter-ego J. Damask writes about werewolves in Singapore. Joyce has also written a sapphic YA fantasy duology with swordsmith clans.

You can also find "Saints & Bodhisattvas" in *Scourge of the Seas of Time (and Space)*, published by Queen of Swords Press.

You can find them at http://awolfstale.wordpress.com and @jolantru.bsky.social on Bluesky. (Pronouns: she/her, they/their).

About Queen of Swords Press

Q UEEN OF SWORDS IS an independent small press, specializing in swashbuckling tales of derring-do, bold new adventures in time and space, mysterious stories of the occult and arcane and fantastical tales of people and lands far and near. Visit us online at www.queenofswordspress.com and sign up for our mailing list to get notified about upcoming releases and offers. Or follow us on social media (@qospress on Bluesky and Instagram) so you don't miss any press news.

If you have a moment, the author would appreciate you taking the time to leave a review for this book at Goodreads, your blog or on the site you purchased it from.

Thank you for your assistance and your support of our authors.